A DEADLY AFFAIR

BOOK SEVEN IN THE GLACIAL BLOOD SERIES

ANNA EDWARDS

Cover Design by www.CharityHendry.com

Logo Design by Charity Hendry

Editing by Tracy Roelle

Formatting by Anna Edwards

Proofreading by: Sheena Taylor

"Because it is my name! Because I cannot have another in my life! Because I lie and sign myself to lies! Because I am not worth the dust on the feet of them that hang! How may I live without my name? I have given you my soul; leave me my name!"

The Crucible - Arthur Miller

FOREWORD

Ever since I was a child, I've been interested in the Wicca world—fascinated by the idea of living off the earth and the existence of magic. I want to believe in magic even though I haven't seen it in reality. It would probably scare the life out of me if I did, but as long as it was used for good, I'd probably fall in love with it.

Suspicion and fear of witchcraft has been used throughout history as an excuse to commit many terrible atrocities. Magic seemed wonderful to me as a little girl until I read 'The Crucible' by Arthur Miller at school, and it broke my heart. The story is set during the time of the Salem witch trials—a dark period in American history. The horrific treatment and punishment of those who stood accused of practicing witchcraft had nothing to do with whether or not they were witches and wizards. The trials were used by many people as an excuse to eliminate the innocent for selfish gain.

However, it wasn't just in Salem the persecution happened, it was all around the world. Where I was born in the county of Essex, UK, there were people killed for being witches—trials were held, and people were hanged. Some were found innocent, but many weren't. Between 1560 and 1675, 760 people were imprisoned, and more often than not, those individuals died from the conditions in the prison. I can't imagine being so scared of something, or rather, so intent on gaining from another's misfortune I'd be willing to subject people to trials like the ones the supposed witches endured.

I wonder what would happen now if we discovered there were people with magical powers in the world? Would the media blow it out of all proportion, and would those exposed be hunted to death? I can't help thinking that might be the case, and I find it sad.

I would love to possess such powers. In fact, my family legend says I do, but I'm unable to access them because I wasn't taught how to by my ancestors for fear of discovery. Maybe my family's magical legacy will be rediscovered one day, but I suspect it won't be in my lifetime. All I can do is hold out hope that my descendants will learn to use their magical gifts, and that when that time comes, they're treated with more respect than those who went before them.

Jessica Raven, the heroine in this story, is forced to hide her abilities because the human race isn't ready to appreciate what she can do, but she's not the most powerful druid in my book. Ciaran has defied all logic and taken great power from darkness. He's made himself unstoppable. He doesn't listen to the goodness in the Earth and uses his sorcery for powerful gain. He's the type of magical being humans should fear, not the kind old lady who used a mixture of herbs to cure a cough and was punished by the Puritans as a consequence.

The world is often back to front, though. For most of us, magic is impossible to comprehend, and it's in our nature to fear the unknown. I only hope the Glacial Blood pack can stop the evil druid before it's too late.

Thank you for reading. I really hope you enjoy this story.

Anna

xx

uka Lincoln sat on a chair in the corner of Ciaran's room. The acrid smell of the druid's potions invaded his nostrils and caused him to cough. He withdrew a handkerchief from the front pocket of his suit jacket and placed it over his nose.

"Will this take much longer?" the alpha polar bear asked his beta, who was currently in the middle of the room, standing in a pentagram drawn on the floor and reciting a spell.

The druid didn't answer, so Nuka reached out with his free hand for the glass of whiskey on the table next to him, and lowering the handkerchief, he took a long sip.

The druid had been in here for hours now, concocting the spell that could change the face of the world forever. The herbs Nuka had obtained from Weston were the last piece of the puzzle. His time was coming soon—he'd rid the world of humans and become the most powerful shifter leader there'd ever been. Hitler would have nothing on him, even though the man did have a great choice in mustache. Nuka stroked under his nose...maybe he should consider growing something like that to distinguish himself from his twin. No, looking the same as Kas would have its advantages when he blamed his brother for everything that was about to happen.

"Ciaran, how much longer?" Nuka tried again, but the druid was lost in the spell.

The chanting stopped, and the air crackled with the intensity of the darkness Ciaran had conjured forth. Black smoke made its way out of the floor in the center of the pentagram and twisted itself around Ciaran's body. Nuka leaned forward. The change had begun. He only hoped Ciaran was strong enough to survive it. He'd never known anyone as well versed in the dark arts as his druid. Jessica, the good witch in the Glacial Blood pack, was weak and feeble compared to his magical man.

"Come on." Nuka found himself chanting as he watched the smoke flood through Ciaran's nostrils into him.

The druid's eyes turned completely black—none of

the iris or the white were visible. Next, a fiery red light enveloped Ciaran and grew brighter and brighter. Nuka shielded his eyes so it wouldn't blind him. But when the room was plunged into darkness, he removed his hand and saw his beta collapsed on the floor. The polar bear got up from his comfortable chair and made his way over to his friend, making sure to avoid stepping inside the pentagram.

"Ciaran. Did it work?"

Nothing.

No movement.

No signs of life.

Fuck.

No.

The druid can't have failed.

Nuka reached out for what appeared to be a witch's broomstick resting against a table. He turned it so the brush end was in his hand, and then making sure he didn't touch any of the chalk pentagram, he prodded at Ciaran with the handle, checking to see if there were any signs of life at all.

Fuck

Shit

Fuck

No.

Nothing.

He gave a much harder prod and jumped back when

Ciaran started to shake, his body going into some kind of a fit. The druid shuddered and shook as fast and as forcefully as a freight train thundering down a track. Nuka stood back when the clothes and black cloak Ciaran was wearing melted from his body and disintegrated into the wooden floor.

"Ciaran?" he tentatively questioned, the broom still held firmly in his hands.

The druid made no answer. The shaking continued at a pace, and Nuka watched with intrigue as the druid's skin color turned green, and brown symbols, like the ones drawn on the walls in Ciaran's room, appeared all over his body.

Nuka took a few more steps back toward the door. Ciaran couldn't tell him what would happen after the spell was cast, because he wasn't sure himself. Nuka knew that the druid was volatile at the moment, though, and the last thing the polar bear wanted was to be caught up in any potential explosion that might occur.

Once Ciaran's body was completely covered in green skin and brown symbols, the fit stopped. The room fell silent for a few seconds before Nuka's beta started to rise from the floor in an unnatural way. He was floating with black smoke cascading from the bottom of his feet. When he was fully upright, Ciaran opened his eyes. They were still as black as the night with no sign of life in them except the darkness of the devil.

Ciaran floated out of the pentagram and toward Nuka. He landed just in front of the polar bear. By the time the druid's feet were firmly planted on the floor, his body had returned to normal without any sign of the green skin, symbols, or black eyes.

"Did it work?" Nuka asked.

Ciaran's lips twisted up into an evil smirk.

"It worked. I possess the magic of darkness—it's more powerful than any other. It's time to bring the fight to the humans and the shifters, starting with the Council headquarters in Berlin and then the prominent leaders of the human world. We'll leave no one alive unless they get down on their knees to us. It's time to reveal the shifters to mankind and move forward with our plan for world domination. No one can stop us now, Nuka. We're invincible."

CHAPTER ONE

"We need to stop this at once. We can't have supernaturals defying our rules. Anyone found breaking these new ones I'm setting out must be brought here and imprisoned."

Ethern watched on as his friend Jürgen, the leader of the shifter Council, read out the new list of rules governing shifters. It was unlikely they would ever be adopted, but at least someone was actively trying to do something. The rest of the Council were running around like headless chickens trying to come up with ways to put a stop to the powerful influence of Nuka Lincoln and his pack. Wiping them out was no longer an option.

In his magical form, Ethern had known the second

the world shifted on its axis a few evenings ago. The powerful blast of dark magic shot through him like an icy blast from the Arctic. It was eerie, unnatural, and scary all at the same time, and everyone with magical abilities felt its effect. Ethern knew exactly where the center of the blast had emanated from, and it scared the life out of him, but he couldn't do anything about it.

"How do you intend to enforce these rules? It's not possible. People are frightened enough as it is. We can't just go around imprisoning everyone we suspect. Have you learned nothing from the witch trials over the centuries? Innocent people will be locked up, and chaos will ensue," another member of the Council challenged.

Ethern slumped back in his chair. He'd heard this argument so many times before. The Council didn't appear to be getting anywhere, and meanwhile, Nuka Lincoln was preparing his next move.

"What would you have me do?" Jürgen questioned their cynical colleague, and Ethern wondered what answer he'd bring to the table. Would it be a fresh perspective on the debate?

"We have to go after the source of the problem," the man replied, thumping the table, and a few people murmured in agreement with him. "It's the only way."

"We don't have the power to go after Nuka Lincoln anymore. You've heard the testimony of the druid community. They are terrified of the power Ciaran possesses now—the magic he wields. We won't be able to fight it, and we won't get anywhere near Nuka until Ciaran is destroyed. We should have acted sooner, but too many people trusted Nuka and his views. In all likelihood, we'll be exposed to the humans before the end of the week, and the fight for our lives will begin. Are you ready for that? Maybe we should be preparing for captivity and death rather than trying to limit what is happening," Jürgen responded, his words passionate but lacking conviction.

Ethern could tell the council leader was defeated. What Jürgen warned the council members about was already here. They'd been lax in protecting the supernaturals. There'd been too many arguments fought out in this room and not enough action taken—that much was obvious to everyone sitting around the table.

Ethern leaned forward in his seat, and as the chair of the meeting, he banged a gavel on the table. Everyone looked toward him with shocked expressions on their faces.

"Jürgen is right. We're too late to stop the war. Whatever Nuka and Ciaran are planning will be here soon. We need to prepare for a future where we'll be under attack and exposed to humans. I would suggest we all return to our home countries and make sure our families and fellow shifter countrymen are protected as best we can. It's all we can do now." Ethern let out a heavy sigh and banged the gavel on the table again. "Meeting closed. We'll reconvene in three days. Hopefully, we'll know more about what's being planned by then, and we can instigate a long-term strategy to counter the harmful effects of exposure."

Pushing back his chair, Ethern stood and bowed his head at his colleagues as they left the room—many of them appeared dejected and full of fear, and all of them were now disappearing back to their homes to make plans for the safety of their loved ones. Ethern didn't need to do that. He would check on his friends in Montana, but he'd lost the one he loved the most when he became a multi-shifter. A different time, and a different life.

The last person to leave the room was Jürgen.

"We've got this all wrong, haven't we?" the leader of the Council questioned Ethern.

"I fear we have. We underestimated Nuka Lincoln and Ciaran's abilities."

"Was it terrible, what you felt?"

Ethern nodded. "Yes, I've experienced several different earthly planes other than this realm, including traveling close to Hell to beg for Selene's life. The darkness there is constricting, choking, and I could barely breathe for the flames surrounding me. That's what I felt when the magic from Ciaran's spell washed over me."

Jürgen looked down at the floor, his eyes shut. The older man was a lion shifter, a once proud creature, but at the moment, he looked defeated.

"Are we certain it was him? That he cast the spell?"

"Yes. Only one druid possesses the skills and strength to create such powerful dark magic. It was foretold."

"It was indeed. It's the reason we sent you to fetch Selene and the rest of the multi-shifters. Everything is a mess, and it's all my fault. I wasn't good enough for this job."

"You've done your best," Ethern tried to reassure his superior, but in his heart, he knew what Jürgen admitted was true.

This wasn't just about shifters anymore. All elements of the supernatural world were involved, and Jürgen didn't possess the understanding to deal with all of that. Ethern had the knowledge, though. For a twenty-seven-year-old man, he'd experienced more than most would in a lifetime, and when this life ended, a new one would start. That was the deal he made with the devil in exchange for Selene's life. He was lucky he'd remain in the shadows, but others wouldn't have the same blessing.

"Go, look after your family, Jürgen. That's the most important thing now."

"Thank you, Ethern."

Jürgen shook his hand, and the two men left the room at the same time. Jürgen walked out, but Ethern's skin turned green with brown symbols, and he used his magical powers to transport himself to the Glacial Blood pack in Montana.

It was quiet when Ethern arrived, eerily so for an area that had been filled with activity over the last few months. He walked into the mansion and called for Kas, the leader of the pack. There was no reply, though. They must be out hunting. He was pleased for them because they needed to stock up on food. Soon, none of them would be able to shift for fear of being caught. The humans were already suspicious of the mansion and its inhabitants, and it would surely be one of the first places to face inspection when Nuka's plan came to fruition.

Two brothers, twins, but so vastly different. There was Kas, the eldest, intent on looking after his pack and offering help to anyone in need, and Nuka, the youngest by just a few short minutes, dead set on killing the humans and ridding the planet of them. How could they be so different? Ethern would never understand what had happened to them in their formative years to make the Lincoln brothers this way. He just had to hold out hope it was Kas, and not Nuka, who was victorious in the coming war.

Instead of searching the rest of the house, Ethern made his way to the room where Jessica Raven, the Glacial Blood witch, practiced her occult arts. If Ciaran was the epitome of evilness, then Jessica was the goddess of all things good. Her spells were cast only to help those around her. He knew she was very close to breaking a magical barrier between the shifters in the Glacial Blood pack and the humans they'd fallen in love with. In animal form, the shifters couldn't communicate with their human counterparts—she was on the verge of finding a way to enable them to do just that.

After quietly entering the room, Ethern stood leaning against a wall and watched Jessica as she performed a spell. He was still in his druid form, and as he listened, he allowed the power of her words to flood into his body.

He'd always admired the ebony-haired witch. Jessica was beautiful as well as having a heart filled with only love and compassion. She didn't know how powerful she was, and it made her all the more special. He'd not dated anyone since he'd become a multi-shifter. It was a higher calling for him, and he needed to concentrate all his efforts on protecting the paranormal community. Romance was a distraction, but lately, as those around him paired up and fell in love, he found Jessica's alluring nature was pulling him closer and closer to her. He couldn't deny it any longer—he wanted her, but she wasn't ready yet. She probably never would be after what Ciaran did to her, so instead, all Ethern could do was protect her and worship her from afar.

Jessica stepped into a pentagram drawn in the center of the room and sat down, cross legged, on the floor. She closed her eyes, and magical words began to leave her mouth and float up into the surrounding air. The words swirled together to form an energy ball above her that glowed and glittered like the brightest diamond. Then, as he watched, the ball transformed into the shape of an animal, that looked a lot like Zain, the honey loving bear shifter from the Glacial Blood pack. Ethern craned his neck and saw two doll poppets lying on the floor in front of Jessica that looked suspiciously like Zain and his new wife, Isobel, who was human. Jessica had to be working again on a spell to enable the two lovers to communicate with each other when Zain was in his animal form. She'd had some success, but so far, the bear and the human could only talk to each other when they were holding hands and Jessica was present with them.

The energy ball transformed from the likeness of Zain to Isobel as Jessica continued to chant. It was fascinating to watch. Ethern really enjoyed being able to explore his magical abilities when he was in witch form, but he'd never be as powerful as Jessica. She was a natural-born vessel for magic. If anyone could match Ciaran for magical skill, it would be her. She just needed to have the confidence to know she'd always remain grounded by her goodness and wouldn't be tempted by the darker side of magic.

The energy flamed brighter and brighter as Jessica's words came out faster and faster. She still hadn't noticed him, and her eyes had turned completely white now—she was immersed in her magic and lost to the human world. Ethern stepped out of his hiding place and closer to her. He knew she would have a magical barrier protecting her, and when he sensed it, he stopped so he didn't alarm her.

He shielded his eyes as the energy ball grew in intensity, becoming white-hot before it exploded into the ether. Jessica gasped for breath and collapsed to the floor within the pentagram. Ethern raced forward in concern, and this time, he triggered the alarm. Jessica rose in an unearthly manner from the floor with energy balls formed in both her hands, ready to attack the intruder.

"Ethern!" The witch's eyes were wide open in shock, and she had a look of fear on her face.

"Are you ok, Jessica?" He asked in concern. "I saw the spell. It looked amazing. Did it work?"

Jessica jumped to her feet, a little unsteadily at first, and he offered his assistance, but she refused it.

"I'm fine, thank you." She brushed herself down. "No, it didn't work. The energy was supposed to project into Zain and Isobel, but instead, it burned up. I need something more."

"Something more? Like what? Do you need help?"

Jessica quickly shook her head. Ethern could sense something was wrong with her.

"What is it?"

"Nothing," she replied abruptly.

He held his hand out and placed it on her shoulder. "Talk to me. What is it?"

"I'll never be able to cast this spell, because it requires something more than I can give. It's not entirely good magic, Ethern. It verges on the dark side, and I won't go there…I can't. Please, leave me alone."

Without another word, Jessica disappeared from the room. She'd said the spell required dark magic, but he couldn't believe that was true when it was intended for such a good purpose. He leaned down and picked the two poppets off the floor. Everything about the Glacial Blood pack was good, so how could it be evil for them to be able to speak to each other in animal and human form? He placed the poppets on a table in the corner of the room by the entrance. If the Glacial Blood couldn't get the magical break they needed to help those who had fallen in love, then what chance did the rest of them have?

He shut his eyes and transported himself to the multi-shifter cave in the Nevada desert where he screamed out his anger and frustration. Maybe he should just hide out here until it was all over, but no, he had a job to do. He immediately teleported back to the Glacial Blood mansion. He needed to be around people.

CHAPTER TWO

Jessica's body was still shaking from the
power that had surged through it while
she was trying to cast her spell. The
magical energy was overwhelming at the end, and she'd
felt the darkness starting to enter her body as she'd
struggled to control it. She was a good witch, a strong
one, and she'd find another way to enable the shifters
and humans to talk to each other whenever they
wanted. Allowing a part of her to slip into the dark side
was not the answer. It was the path to losing herself,
and she could never let that happen.

She'd transported directly from the room she used
for her magic into her bedroom and collapsed on the
bed. Her entire body was aching with tiredness. The
spell had required a lot of effort, and in spite of every-

thing, it still hadn't worked. It was frustrating and upsetting. She desperately wanted to give this gift to her friends, and it looked increasingly like she wouldn't be able to do it.

Closing her eyes, she allowed sleep to overtake the thoughts whirring around in her mind.

Jessica knocked loudly on the door to her new professor's room. She was nervous as hell but also felt lucky to be here at the prestigious Westridge Academy in California. It was the only magic school she'd ever wanted to attend, not that there were many of them to choose from in the world. Magic existed only in the shadows and probably always would.

Westridge was the best of the best, though. The teachers possessed amazing abilities and had knowledge of spells capable of winning wars. She wanted to learn everything and become one of the most powerful witches in the world.

At three years old, when she started inventing spells to reduce the time her mother spent on household chores, her parents had told her she was destined for great things. In truth, she'd created the spells for purely selfish reasons—if her mom was busy cooking and cleaning, there was less time for them to play with Jessica's dolls.

When she'd got the letter to say she'd been accepted at the school, she was overjoyed. She was eighteen years old, and today was the start of the rest of her life. Everything that had come before was simply preparing her for this moment.

She stepped back from the door and waited to be given

permission to enter. Everyone knew in magic school you never walked into a room without being invited. It could mean you ended up being turned into a frog or worse if the druid inside was doing a spell.

"Enter," a stern voice called out to her, and she tentatively pushed the door open.

Ciaran Dunaid was one of the youngest tutors at the school, only a few years older than her, but she'd heard fantastic things about him from the other students. Some said he was the best tutor, and she was lucky he was her mentor.

She'd been on edge all morning in advance of their appointment. Now as she stood in front of the druid, she couldn't help but think how handsome he was with his strong jawline and dark hair. He looked down at her with his deep brown eyes full of magic and wonder. The stern expression on his face only added to his charm.

"Miss Raven, I've been expecting you!" Ciaran exclaimed, and she held her hand out to him.

"Thank you for taking me on as your student, sir. I read all the texts you sent me over the summer. I have lots of questions, but then I'm sure that's why you sent them, to get my brain working."

She was babbling like a love struck schoolgirl, but the texts he'd sent her had truly been amazing. They'd captured her imagination and left her wondering about so many aspects of the magical world. There was a lot to learn, and she'd jotted all her questions down in the thick notebook currently weighing down her small backpack.

"That is good. I'm glad my texts gave you something to think about, and we'll discuss all your questions in the next tutorial. But for today's session, even though I know you demonstrated your skills in the entrance exams, I want to see your abilities for myself."

"Of course, sir."

Ciaran motioned for her to take a seat on a nearby chair. He was dressed in a dark t-shirt and black jeans that matched the décor of the room they were in. The walls were painted black, and the light was blocked out by dark curtains. The only illumination came from candles on the walls. It seemed strange—the building they were in was very modern, equipped with the latest technological advancements, but her tutor's room had an old world vibe to it, complete with cobwebs and leather-bound books lining the walls. She liked it because it suggested to her that Ciaran was passionate about his art rather than just teaching because it was his way of earning money.

"Right." Ciaran pulled a book from the thousands on the shelves and handed it to her. "Have you heard of this book?"

She looked down at the title.

"Yes, sir. 'The Divination'. It's supposed to contain some of the oldest spells known to man."

Ciaran nodded.

"It does. I want you to open to page two hundred and thirty-seven, please."

She quickly scrambled to find the correct page.

"To call forth energy," she read out to him.

"Yes." He perched on a table filled with more books and bottles of herbs—some of the herbs were preserved in liquid, and others looked fresh like they'd been recently plucked from a bush. "Well, come on then, I'm waiting."

She looked at him in confusion until she realized he meant for her to cast the spell.

"Sorry," she exclaimed and immediately launched into reading out loud the spell from the book.

With her hand held out in front of her, she called forth a ball of energy to form in her palm. Pushing off from where he was perched, Ciaran came over to her. She looked up at him, his alluring presence strangled the breath in her throat. Was her energy ball all right? Was it big enough? Bright enough? She was suddenly nervous, and when he leaned down and whispered into her ear, she flushed with heat.

"Don't be scared of me, Jessica. I can show you amazing things. Wonders you never knew existed. Trust me."

Standing upright again, he held his hand over the energy ball, and it crystallized in her hands, transformed into a beautiful solid mass of glass in a myriad of swirling colors. It felt heavy, and she reached her other hand up to hold it steady.

"It's stunning. How did you do that?"

"Magic." Ciaran laughed. "Turn to page one hundred and five," he ordered.

She disintegrated the glass ball into the ether and reached for the book again. The spell she was now given allowed her to change her form. She liked the idea, but she hadn't used this spell much, because she didn't feel the need to alter how she looked.

Where she used to live, there'd been a young female witch who'd performed the spell on herself when she went into puberty. As a result, she didn't get acne or any of the oddities that came with a growing body, but it seemed wrong. Jessica wasn't a stunning beauty, not in her eyes anyway—she had a bit of weight in places she'd rather not, and at certain times of the month, she felt like chopping all her long, black hair off because it wouldn't do what she asked of it. However, it felt wrong to mess with her appearance.

"Have you done this one before? It didn't say on your report." Ciaran resumed his vantage point, sat on the edge of his table.

"It wasn't required in my exam, but I have used it before. Not often, though. What would you like me to change into?"

Ciaran stroked his chin in thought.

"Show me your appearance if you were a man."

She giggled. She'd done this before. She'd been curious about the male anatomy and had transformed herself. She could see why men were obsessed with the length between their legs. She'd had a play with hers. It was fun.

"Something I should know?" Ciaran raised an eyebrow at her.

"No, sir. I'll change now."

She knew this spell so didn't need to read it from the book. Shutting her eyes, she imagined herself as a man: a fuller face, more muscles, shorter hair, and taller. She felt her body changing, and when she opened her eyes again, her voice had developed a masculine edge.

"Is this all right, sir?"

"Excellent, although I think I prefer you as a woman."

Her tutor winked at her, and she felt her body heat as the appendage between her legs hardened a little. She quickly cancelled the spell and returned to being a female.

"Much better," Ciaran said, smiling at her, and this time, she felt warmth pool between her thighs.

What was going on? The room suddenly felt very hot. She couldn't have a crush on her tutor. She was here to learn and nothing else. She took a deep breath to compose herself.

"Page ten," Ciaran called out this time, and she jumped out of her skin, trying to calm her overactive libido as she flicked to the page required.

Her heart instantly sank—she didn't like this spell. It had never sat right with her. Ciaran reached out and grabbed a lump of coal from his table and placed it before her.

"One of the simplest spells, but not many people approve of it. I want you to turn this coal into a diamond," he ordered.

She wasn't sure why she didn't like this spell—it was

entry level standard, but it just felt wrong to her. It seemed stupid to teach it to those with magical powers when it could so easily be used for financial gain. Druids were taught humility—it was a fundamental part of who they were. They didn't want the wealth or power it required to take over the world. They just wanted to live frugally off the earth and be free.

"Is something wrong?" Ciaran asked.

As she debated the spell, he'd moved, so he was now standing immediately in front of her.

"No, sir," she quickly answered.

"You're hesitating? Is something wrong with this spell?"

"Will I turn the diamond back after?"

"If you want to, but I do have plenty more coal." He waved his hand around the room, pointing out several other lumps of the black rock. "I do have the same reluctance as you, though. If I decided to take over the world, I wouldn't conjure up a load of diamonds to make the money I needed. I would do it with a bit more class. Every time a student doesn't change it back, I turn it to coal again myself when they leave."

She nodded, grateful for his understanding.

Saying the spell aloud, she changed the coal to a bright shining diamond, and as soon as Ciaran acknowledged she'd completed the task, she quickly changed the diamond back to coal.

"Well done." He was still standing directly in front of her,

and she could smell his musky aftershave in her nostrils. "Do you know what happens to the students who don't turn the diamond back?"

She shook her head, not realizing it was part of the test as well.

"No, sir."

"I refuse to have them as my students any longer. Congratulations, you've passed."

An overwhelming sense of elation washed over her, and she jumped up from her seat and threw her arms around him.

"Thank you, thank you."

She was so happy at hearing this news she didn't realize what she was doing until Ciaran's lips met hers in a passionate kiss. She melted into his arms and allowed herself to be caught up in what was happening—it felt so right.

She'd only just arrived at Westridge, and she was already learning in more ways than one, and these lessons would shape her future forevermore.

CHAPTER THREE

"Scott, save some for the rest of us." Brayden, the beta of the Glacial Blood pack, moaned when his blond haired, lion shifter friend pulled the whole leg off the deer in front of them.

Ethern sat quietly at the dining table munching on the slice of meat he'd been given by Brayden's mom, Jane. She'd cooked a portion of the venison for those who preferred their meat less…well, raw. Jessica and Isobel screwed up their faces in disgust at the lion shifter—they were both vegetarians. Ethern had tried it for a while, but he loved meat too much.

"How did the spell practice go?" Isobel asked Jessica, and the raven haired witch shook her head, informing her friend it hadn't gone well. Isobel looked sad. "Don't worry, Jessica. I'm sure you'll get it soon. I'm in awe of what you can do. I wish I had some sort of special power, but alas, I'm just a regular human."

"But a sexy one." Zain wrapped his arms around his wife and pulled her closer to him.

The bear shifter was eating salmon instead of the venison. Isobel screwed up her face when he kissed her.

"You taste of fish," she complained, but Zain just winked at her—a private joke going on between them.

Ethern enjoyed watching the interactions between the pack. In spite of the pressure on them, they were all relaxed and enjoying the meal. It was always the same way with them. When it came to a fight, they were there supporting each other, and downtime was no different. They enjoyed being here all together. He'd never been part of a pack and wondered what it would be like. The Council wasn't a pack by any means, just a collective of people who were currently trying to find a way to stop war coming but failing badly.

"Scott," Brayden shouted again when the lion went to retrieve yet more meat.

"But I'm hungry," the lion protested and looked pitifully at his wife, the lioness shifter, Emma.

She was holding one of their twins to her breast, feeding the infant at the same time as eating her own meal. The other twin rested in the arms of Selene, Brayden's partner and a multi-shifter like Ethern.

Selene's pregnancy bump was getting big now and the arrival of her baby was imminent. No one had any idea how long her gestation would be. No multi-shifter had ever had a child before, so it was all a matter of guesswork.

"Brayden, stop moaning at Scott," Selene scolded her husband playfully. "You know how hungry he gets."

"How he stays so skinny, I'll never know." Brayden shook his head and pulled another whole leg off the deer to eat.

Kas, the leader of the Glacial Blood pack, sat at the head of the table, watching everything happening around him. He looked tired, and Ethern knew the polar bear shifter had been having nightmares since finding out his grandfather had been brought back to life by Nuka.

"Thank you for inviting me to dinner," Ethern expressed his gratitude to Kas.

"It's ok." Kas gave him a small smile. "I apologize for the rest of the company, though."

"Hey," a few of the other shifters complained, but Kas simply returned to his seal blubber—his favorite meat, courtesy of Jane.

The rest of the meal continued in this vein. Lots of teasing and playful retorts between the assembled pack. By the end of it, Ethern felt relaxed and happy. The stress of the earlier Council meeting had dissipated, and he resolved to forget about it until tomorrow.

Jessica excused herself from the table, and Ethern watched as she disappeared back into her magic room. He took his leave and followed her. When he entered the room, she looked up at him.

"I'm not going to try the spell again if that's what you've come to ask me," she announced with a rather abrupt tone to her voice.

"I'm not," he responded, moving closer to her. "I know you'll do the spell in your own time. You don't need pressure from me. I'm sorry for earlier."

Jessica nodded. "I'm sorry for disappearing the way I did earlier. It was rude. I was feeling defeated and exhausted. I just wanted some time to myself and to sleep for a bit. It would be amazing for the others to be able to speak to each other in both human and animal form, I hate that I can't help them. Lily, Hunter and Kingsley have really benefited from it."

Ethern knew Jessica had helped another set of their friends who belonged to a different pack in Kansas. Hunter, a wolf shifter and alpha of his pack, had a loving partnership with Lily, a bear shifter, and Kingsley, a human. However, the three had encountered a number of difficulties early on in their relationship, and Jessica had used her powers to help the triad overcome some of those challenges by enabling them to communicate freely together in all their forms.

"You will get there. Jessica. Your magical abilities are amazing. I learn something new every time I watch you."

Ethern was in awe of her skills. His own magical abilities had come to him because he touched a witch, and he didn't know how to use them like Jessica did. Most of the magic he did manage was a matter of guesswork and following his instincts. Whereas Jessica had practiced for so many years now it had become second nature to her.

"Thank you." Jessica bit her lip, and Ethern found himself reaching out to touch her on the shoulder.

"Trust me."

"I do, Ethern. I lost my way for a while, but my confidence in my abilities is growing again. I do worry, though. Sometimes the power surging through me is so strong I fear losing myself to it."

"I think we all do. You're probably unaware, but multi-shifters possess a power that could leave us lost to all we know if it's not controlled. The most important thing is to trust yourself and those around you to keep you grounded."

"I often forget my support network is one of the strongest in the supernatural world. The things some of those people in the other room have been through are so shocking—I can't imagine coming out the other side and then being able to laugh and joke about the world at large while sitting down for a meal."

Ethern let go of Jessica and picked up the book she'd been looking at. He flicked through the pages as he thought about how to respond to her.

"The Glacial Blood pack is like no other. It's an inclusive mix of shifters and humans and an example of what the world could be like without intolerance. I may not be a member, but I'm glad I'm allowed to be a part of it even in a very small way."

Jessica took the book from him.

"I wouldn't say you're not a member of the pack. It's unofficial, but you're with us when we need you."

"Thank you. I would do anything for my friends here."

Jessica looked up at him, and the air heated in the room. Was he overthinking it, or did she have feelings for him as well? They fell silent for a few moments while Jessica stepped away and began to look through the book in her hands.

"Let's cast a spell together, Ethern. I've got one I'm not sure you know. I want to try it with you."

"Ok." He chuckled and allowed his skin to display the green hue and markings of a witch.

Jessica lifted her gaze from the book and took in his new appearance.

"I would love to see my true form one day. I'm jealous multi-shifters get to change and I don't" she said wistfully, tentatively reaching out and tracing the pentagram tattoo on his hand. " I wonder what symbols I'd have. You and Selene both have different markings, and I don't even recognize some of them. It's intriguing."

"I agree. It's a fascinating ancient language. I don't know the meaning of a lot of the markings, but I feel them when I use my magic. Each one gives me a different power." He pointed to a small star on his face just beneath his left eye. "This one is where my teleportation comes from. It heats up whenever I teleport."

"The wandering star." Jessica reached up to touch the small tattoo on his face. "Maybe when the war is over, we can spend some time exploring them. See what they do?"

Ethern fell quiet. He knew already he wouldn't end the war in this form. Sacrifices had to be made, and it was the reason why he'd been raised from the dead as a multi-shifter.

"Anyway," he said, changing the subject. "What is this spell?"

Jessica handed the book back to him and pointed at a page. He started to read while she began searching around on her desk for something. The spell was a little mundane, turning coal to a diamond. It seemed a silly spell to him and had the potential of being a dangerous one if it fell into the wrong hands. Jessica handed him a lump of coal. He looked down at it like it was burning his hands.

"Why this spell?" he asked.

"It's different, and it's good way to practice when learning to change the shape and properties of objects."

Jessica placed her hand over the coal, and it changed into a spectacular diamond. It took his breath away with its beauty. He looked at it more closely, admiring the line of the precious stone. Its cut was exquisite and its carat would be very high. It would be worth a fortune. He looked up and noticed Jessica was watching him intently, her brows deeply furrowed in the center of her forehead.

She placed her hand over the stone again, and it turned back into a lump of coal.

"Your turn," Jessica challenged as she started to walk away from him.

Her shoulders were slumped, and if he guessed correctly, she was deflated and worried about something.

"Jessica, wait." He stopped her with his free hand. "What's wrong?"

"Your turn," she repeated, her voice cracking as she spoke.

She pulled away from him and took a seat on a

nearby chair while he stared down at the lump of coal. This was a test. He felt it deep inside. He didn't want to turn the lump of sedimentary rock into a diamond. It wasn't him. Precious stones weren't what he wanted or even needed in his life. Money had no value to him.

He felt a burning on his back from another of his tattoos, and he gasped causing Jessica's eyes to widen. He knew exactly which marking it was—the one of a black raven. He placed his free hand over the lump of coal and allowed the magic within him to work. When he pulled his hand away, instead of a diamond there was a black feather resting in his hand—a large tail feather of a raven. Walking over to Jessica, he handed it to her.

"I don't need diamonds. This raven's feather is of more value to me than anything else. It represents all that's in my heart."

Jessica opened her mouth to speak, to respond to him but then clamped it shut again. She looked down at the feather, and a tear fell from her eye.

"Goodnight, my sweet raven," Ethern said softly, knowing it was time to leave. He'd told her the truth, but she wasn't ready.

He allowed the star on his cheek to heat and transported himself back to the multi-shifters' cave in Nevada. What happened next was up to her.

CHAPTER FOUR

The black raven's feather sat in Jessica's hand. She couldn't stop looking down at the fraying tendrils from the mystical bird that matched her surname, and she favored as her symbol. Ethern had feelings for her. She'd suspected it for a long time but had never wanted to face it. Her heart had been broken once before, and she wasn't sure it would ever be truly repaired. She didn't trust easily, and Ethern would probably end up hating her in the long term as a result. It was better to stay alone and focus on her magic. She didn't need the love of a man. She had her family, the Glacial Blood pack, and their love and support for her was unwavering.

She placed the feather down on the table in front of

her and teleported herself to her bedroom. It was late, and the sounds of the other couples settling down echoed around the tall ceiling in her room. Kas growled loudly and the noise quietened a little. Jessica chuckled. You didn't argue with a tired polar bear if you had any sense.

She got herself ready for bed and climbed in-between the crisp cotton sheets. There were several books of magic on her nightstand, and she knew she should study some more spells, but she was too exhausted from the day. It'd been one that taxed her mind more than anything else. She settled down in her bed, and raising her hand, she firmly pressed the center of her forehead with her finger. A magical glow flowed from her and cocooned her body in a safety blanket.

"Sleep," she stated, and the world fell black.

Jessica had been at the school for nine months now. She'd spent almost every day of that with Ciaran, and they'd fallen in love with each other. During the day they'd practice magic spells in his office, and at night they'd explore each other's bodies in his bed. She was in heaven.

This was the life she wanted, and she couldn't wait for the future. Ciaran had hinted at marrying her when she'd finished her studies. She knew it was wrong to be in a relationship with her tutor, and they always had to be careful around the other staff members. However, they were both consenting adults, so in her mind, it didn't matter. There was only a few weeks left of school before she could begin the rest of her life with Ciaran at her side.

His ideas were insane at times. He believed in a future where magic could be used freely. She longed for it but also knew that while the humans remained ignorant of the existence of magic they were all safer. She still supported Ciaran in his endeavors and was amazed by some of the spells he'd managed to perform. A few swayed a little to the darker side than she felt comfortable with, but he was strong, and as long as they had love in their hearts, she was confident they'd keep each other grounded.

"I can't believe you're going to be doing the end of year spell." *Gracie, Jessica's best friend at Westridge, jumped up and down excitedly.*

"I know," *Jessica replied, smiling at her friend.*

She'd been practicing this particular spell for months. At first, she'd been awful at it, but the spell allowed her to resurrect dead animals, so she'd persevered. She'd kept trying to revive rabbits caught in traps and not too damaged roadkill until finally she'd had a breakthrough with the spell last week. Floppy, as she called the resurrected rabbit, was now happily living in a cage in Ciaran's office.

She was confident she had the skills to be a powerful druid, possibly one of the best, although not as great as Ciaran of course. She could never exceed his powers—they were beyond superb.

"What are you going to bring back to life at the graduation ceremony?" Gracie questioned. She was a talented witch herself but not as good as Jessica.

"I don't know. I'll have to see what I can find." Jessica leaned into her friend and whispered, "Ciaran was joking the other day. He said we should dig up one of the old headmasters buried in the graveyard at the back of the school and bring him back to life."

Gracie squealed and then grasped her hands over her mouth.

"You wouldn't, would you? Oh my god, Jessica, you have to. It would be fantastic. You'll go down in history at the school. The greatest graduate ever."

Jessica shook her head.

"No, I'm not going to mess around with things like that. Animals I can do because they shouldn't have died the way they did, at the hands of humans. The headmasters are different. They died of old age—their deaths were natural. Bringing them back would be wrong and it would interfere with the order of life. Besides, the spell for supernatural resurrection is so hard I don't think I could do it even if I tried."

"I bet you could. You can do anything when it comes to magic. You're insanely gifted as a druid, Jessica. I can't do half the stuff you can." Gracie puffed out her lips. "My future won't be saving the Earth. I'm not sure where I'll end up. I'm no good at anything."

"You're an excellent witch, Gracie," Jessica reassured her friend. "If nothing else, we can both stay here and be teachers. I'm sure Ciaran could arrange it."

"I bet he could. Maybe I'll have a word." Gracie giggled just as the bell rang for classes to start.

Gracie had a free period now, but Jessica had potions. She found the subject boring because she knew most of the potions from her tutelage at the hands of Ciaran. She needed to attend the class, though, for her graduation points.

"See you later, Gracie."

She waved to her friend as she grabbed the books she needed and made her way into the nearby classroom. It was emptier than normal with only a handful of students. She approached the teacher, an old lady named Mrs. Wickread.

"Where is everyone, Mrs. Wickread?"

The teacher rolled her eyes in annoyance.

"Apparently the head has given leave to half of my class to practice for the end of year show. I wish she'd told me sooner. I wouldn't have bothered spending hours doing a lesson plan." Mrs. Wickread handed Jessica a sheet of paper. "I've given everyone here this sheet. Once you've made the potion on it, you can go. I'm not going to waste my time doing a full lesson. Most of the students attending class today already know what they're doing. They're the ones who've actually studied. They don't want to be druids just to throw energy balls at each other."

It took Jessica no time at all to make the potion, and after showing it to Mrs. Wickread, she was dismissed. She wasn't due to have her lesson with Ciaran for another half an hour, but she couldn't think of anything else except going to see him. Maybe they could have a quickie before practicing more spells. She made her way through the corridor at a fast pace to Ciaran's office.

Forgetting to knock with her excitement, the cardinal rule of wizardry in the school, she barged into his room. Her world shifted. Her mouth fell open at the sight in front of her —Ciaran naked with Gracie on his lap. They were having sex, and not in a missionary position like she and Ciaran normally did.

The man she thought she would marry and her best friend were cheating on her. Bile pooled in her stomach as Ciaran looked up to see her standing at the door.

"Fuck," he exclaimed and tossed Gracie unceremoniously onto the floor.

Jessica's best friend protested until she saw what Ciaran was looking at.

"Shit!" Gracie swore and quickly tried to cover herself.

"Jessica, come here," Ciaran ordered her, but she didn't move—her feet rooted themselves to the floor.

"How could you?" Tears pooled in her eyes.

"Come here," Ciaran commanded again, this time more forcefully, and she felt her body move through the air.

"Let me go," Jessica pleaded, but she was too tightly

wrapped in whatever spell Ciaran was using on her. She didn't recognize the man she loved. He was naked in front of her, but he was like a different person. His eyes were dark as he pulled her flush against him. "How could you, Ciaran? I love you."

The edges of his mouth twisted up into a sadistic smile.

"Just what I wanted you to feel for me. It allows me to feed on your magic."

"What do you mean?"

She couldn't believe what she was hearing. Had she fallen into an alternate reality at some point in the day?

"Poor naïve, Jessica. So unaware of the power you possess. The power I've been feeding off ever since you walked into this room nine months ago. It was the only reason I fucked you. You're a crap lay. Nothing about you excites me. You're boring and so sanctimonious."

Ciaran placed his hand on her forehead, and she felt her whole body tighten.

"What are you doing?"

Ciaran licked his lips.

"I've found a new toy to play with. It's time to take the last dregs of power I can from you and move on."

Who was this man? He was nothing like the man she'd fallen in love with. He was a demon—a dark magic had possessed him. She had to help him.

"Ciaran, please remember the love we share. This is just dark magic talking. It's not you. Don't allow it to win."

Ciaran let out a bellowing laugh.

"You really are naïve, Jessica. Dark magic possessed me long before you ever walked into this room."

Patterns started to swirl around her head. Her magic was leaving her. No, she couldn't lose her abilities. They were everything to her. She was going to be a powerful, good witch and help bring peace to the world. How could she have been so stupid? Was she that desperate for love?

She summoned a strength from somewhere deep down inside her and focused on a remote location away from Westridge. The highest mountain, the coldest place, some-where she could hide and never be found—a park she adored from the holidays of her youth in Montana. She had to act quickly.

She recited words from a long since memorized spell, and Ciaran's hold over her broke as a blanket of protective energy encased her. She took one last look at the man who'd not only broken her heart but shattered it. He'd taken everything from her, and she knew she'd never trust a man again. Love was off limits to her.

The darkness of the room disappeared. All around her was snow, and the sky above her was a vibrant, bright blue. She'd escaped. Her head flopped down into her hands, and she let the tears flow until she heard a soft growl. When she jerked her head up, a polar bear stood in front of her. She'd escaped from one monster and landed straight into the jaws of another, except she sensed something different about this one. She reached out and placed her hand on his head. The polar bear let her, and she heard his deep voice inside her head.

"Hello, I'm Kas Lincoln. Welcome to the Glacial Blood pack."

CHAPTER FIVE

The magical power that surged through Ciaran was almost overwhelming, but he was more than capable of controlling it. He longed to test out his new strength and was growing impatient, waiting for Nuka to decide on the target. The druid reached his arm out to the left and energy swirled all around him. It crackled in the silent air.

"If you damage anything, you'll be fixing it straight after," Nuka growled.

Ciaran allowed his lips to twist up into a playful smile before sending a bolt of energy into the wall. It ripped a hole right through the brickwork, so they could see outside to the freshly fallen snow of the morning. Nuka growled again, and Ciaran pulled the energy back, repairing the wall as he did so.

"Why don't you go and fuck something to utilize your energy?" Nuka puffed out a frustrated breath.

"I don't even need to fuck to get off now. I just have to think about it, and I'm coming like a freight train." Ciaran raised an eyebrow at his alpha.

"I really didn't need to know that, Ciaran."

"Sounds a lot better to me. Women are only good for sucking dick. If men could get the same satisfaction without them, then maybe we could rid the world of them as well. Less nagging that way." Nuka's grandfather joined in the conversation.

Nuka's grandfather currently looked like himself , but Ciaran could feel Samuel lingering in the room. Samuel was the human ex-councilman who'd allowed his body to be used as the vessel to resurrect Nuka's elderly relative.

"Women stay." Nuka grunted and got to his feet. "As Ciaran here is feeling a need to test his new-found powers, I say we give the world a show it's never seen before. Who's with me?"

"What do you have in mind?" Ciaran subdued the powerful dark energy cascading within his body.

"I think a little trip to Germany is in order," Nuka announced with an evil smirk, full of malevolence.

"I couldn't think of a better place to start the war." Nuka's grandfather agreed and stood up.

All three joined hands, and Ciaran transported them

away from Canada, where they lived, to the headquarters of the supernatural Council at the Reichstag in Berlin. The Council primarily dealt with the shifters of the world, but it imposed rules on anyone who was not of full human blood.

A few humans noticed them appear and ran for their lives, screaming as they went. Ciaran immediately silenced them with bolts of energy that cut them down dead.

"Leave the humans for now," Nuka ordered. "They're not our main target here." Nuka raised his hand and pointed directly at the Reichstag building. "That is."

"And what exactly do you want me to do with it?" Ciaran questioned, rubbing his hands together in gleeful anticipation.

"Bring it to the ground, Ciaran. I want it destroyed. I want the Council members dead. Without them, the shifter world will seek a new leader, and that's where I'll step in."

Ciaran could tell Nuka was almost buzzing with excitement—finally, he was witnessing the culmination of all the years of hard work.

"I'm more than happy to oblige."

They walked closer to the building. Nuka stood in the center of the three of them in his tailored suit, his grandfather was to the left in slacks and an open necked shirt, and Ciaran was on the right. He was in his usual all black attire. The druid rose from the ground and floated through the air, wanting to put on a show no one could forget. His eyes turned as black as the night sky, and the magic swirled around him. A few of the people who worked in the building rushed forward, trying to stop him, but Ciaran shot bolts of black energy straight through them. He ignited their bodies in bright orange flames and watched on as they burned to a painful death.

"Nice!" Nuka exclaimed beside him. "I might have to put you in charge of hunting game in the future. Flame grilled is my favorite."

"Done." Ciaran chuckled and shot off a few more bolts of black energy.

He recognized one of the men who bore down on them—he was a senior member of the Council. This time, Ciaran allowed green energy to flow from him. It wrapped around the man, coiling tighter and tighter like a snake preparing to devour its prey. The man's eyes bulged as he choked and gagged for breath until Ciaran threw his head back with a laugh and ripped the green energy through the man's body, tearing him into thousands of tiny pieces of bleeding flesh, bone, and organs on the ground.

"This is better than watching TV." Nuka's grandfather applauded the show Ciaran was putting on.

"I don't know. I think it will be on all the television channels tonight. Headline news—the war is here." Nuka pointed out where a few humans were filming what was happening.

"Well then, I better give the media something fascinating to overreact to."

Ciaran floated higher into the sky. People stepped back, looks of horror on their faces, as he allowed the darkness within him to fully take control. He shot bolts of red energy from his hands, slamming them hard into the walls of the Reichstag. They shook the building. Windows shattered, and fires spontaneously broke out.

Next, he held his hands out in front of him. He turned his palms upward and started to lift the building from its very foundation. Humans and supernaturals jumped from the windows. Those who were able to change to flying animals did so to escape, but others fell to their deaths. Panic and chaos ensued as he lifted the building higher and higher. The entire of Berlin came to a standstill with everyone looking up at the grand, old building dominating the sky and casting dark ominous shadows over the ground.

Ciaran shut his eyes and wrapped Nuka's grandfather and Nuka in a protective shield before opening his eyes again as he turned his palms face down. The building fell from a height of at least a few thousand feet in the air and slammed down, sending bricks, dust, and bodies scattering everywhere. It created a crater in the ground so wide it looked like a meteorite had struck the Earth.

Ciaran floated back down to the ground and admired his handiwork, the flattened Reichstag building no longer recognizable as the headquarters of the Council.

"Was that the sort of show you wanted?" he asked Nuka.

"I can't think of anything you could've done better. Let's go home and celebrate. You can use your magic to make yourself come, but I'm going to do it the old-fashioned way and find a warm pussy to fuck."

Ciaran laughed and transported them away from the chaos of sirens and death in Berlin,

"I think I'll give women another try."

CHAPTER SIX

*E*thern woke from the darkness that had claimed him when the building started shaking. He could feel the heat of fires burning close by, but the world was dark all around him. When the building had started to lift into the air, he'd changed from his human form into an ant. At the time, it had been the smallest animal he could think of that had strength enough to support more than its own body weight.

What the hell had happened?

His magical side had sensed the overwhelming power coming from outside before the building had started to rise from the ground, but he'd not been able to stop it. The magic was too strong, and that could mean only one thing…Ciaran was responsible.

Ethern moved as quickly as he could away from the pile of rubble he was taking shelter under. Everything surrounding him had crumbled into nothing. Steel supports jutted out at odd angles, and bodies littered the floor—Jürgen's was one of them. Had anyone survived? The building or what was left of it was fragile. He used his animal senses as an ant to crawl toward safety. Eventually, after what seemed like a lifetime, he emerged into the dusty air of Berlin.

Ensuring no one was watching him, he shifted back into his human form and looked up at what remained of the building. He was right. It was little more than a pile of rubble. He fell to the floor, the shock of what had happened overwhelming him. People moved all around him—humans and shifters in a panic while medics desperately tried to save the lives of people with severe injuries. Humans huddled together in horror and whispered of a fearful demon being the cause—a man with black eyes and magical energy. His suspicions were confirmed…Ciaran was responsible.

What would happen now?

He took a few moments longer to compose himself, a ringing continued in his ears from the collapse of the building. If he hadn't changed form and found a safe place to hide, he would be one of the bodies inside. He got to his feet unsteadily. The insane shifters in the basement were his first worry. He had to make sure none of them had escaped, but it was then he noticed the crater surrounding him. When the building fell, they would have all been killed instantly. There was no hope for any of them. Thankfully, he'd taken their greatest weapon out of the dungeon a few weeks earlier.

"Ethern, thank god," a voice called him, but he couldn't place where it was coming from until a hand touched his shoulder.

One of the junior members of the Council stood before him. He was covered in blood.

"Are you hurt?" Ethern's immediate urge was to change to a witch to help the young man.

"I'm fine. It's not my blood." The man started to lead Ethern away from the building to where a makeshift medical area was being set up.

"Thank goodness you're ok." Ethern struggled for breath in the dusty air around him. "What happened?"

"Ciaran," the man whispered quietly and jerked his head in the direction of the crowds of gathered journalists. "I was returning from lunch and saw everything. He lifted the building from the ground and then dropped it. Everyone else saw it too. We're exposed. The war...it's finally here."

Ethern felt the bile pool in his throat. Ciaran had

used his magic in a dramatic and bone-chilling way in full view of the humans. There would be no way of hiding what had happened. It would be impossible to get rid of all the pictures flooding around the world at this very moment. It was over. Life, as the supernatural world knew it, was about to change.

"Was it only magic?" Ethern asked, desperately hoping there were some limitations to the damage he would have to control.

The junior councilman was a leopard shifter, and Ethern could see he was worried about exposure.

"Yes, it was, I think. No one changed. Well, a few of the bird shifters did, but I don't think anyone saw them do it. Ciaran was with Nuka and another older man I didn't recognize, and they all stayed in human form."

"That's a blessing. At least, it's just magic we have to worry about at the moment."

"It's all such a mess." The young leopard shifter looked over at the ruined building. The medics were covering the dead with sheets—some bodies were charred, and some were broken from falling. Blood ran into the gutters. It was the site of a massacre. "What do we do now, sir?"

"What do you mean?" Ethern shook his head, not really understanding the question.

The leopard shifter gulped. "The Council is gone. You and I, plus a few of the bird shifters, are the only ones to have survived. Everyone else was in the building. They're all dead. You're our leader as the most senior person still alive."

"Dead." Ethern's breath caught again, his head began to spin. It couldn't be. Dear god, Nuka had taken the whole Council, leaving the shifters without a governing body and giving him the opportunity to become their leader when fear took over. He was insane. "I...er..."

Ethern tried to focus his thoughts, but all he could see was death and destruction until a familiar hand placed its protecting warmth on his shoulder. Jessica's healing energy flooded through his body, giving him the ability to think straight again. When he turned to look at her, she had tears in her eyes and was staring at the demolished building.

"I sensed Ciaran's magic," she stumbled over her words, emotion coursing through her body at seeing the atrocity before her, no doubt.

Ethern got to his feet. His senses returned.

"He's killed everyone in the Council," Ethern informed her. "Well, nearly everyone. There are a few still alive."

"This is what I feared."

"We need to get the survivors out of here and get them somewhere safe. Nuka will come for them. Anyone who can stop his power is now a threat."

"Yes." Jessica finally shifted her gaze from the building to him. "I thought you were dead."

He shook his head, allowing a weary smile to cross his face.

"The joy of being a multi-shifter. I can make myself small and strong."

"I'm glad." Jessica bit her lip.

Ethern took her hand and squeezed it to give her reassurance. He was in effect the leader now, and he wouldn't allow the shifters to be destroyed by Nuka. He needed to make plans and work to save them all.

"Jessica, I need your help. Can you take the survivors back to the Glacial Blood mansion? We'll find a better hiding place soon, but for now, I just want them away from here. There's a lot of sensitive information inside the building, including some old texts. I need to find them and get them away from here before the humans start the recovery and clearing up process."

Jessica nodded.

"What about the bodies of the shifters in the dungeons?" she asked.

"Magic destroyed this building, and I'm going to have to use it again to protect as many of our secrets as I can."

"You're going to incinerate their remains."

"I have to. I'll do anything I can to make sure we're

not discovered. If we can mitigate what is happening here, maybe it won't be as bad. Ciaran has captured the attention of the world, but I won't let him have the last say and push everyone into Nuka's way of thinking. Go, please, the pair of you. We need to do this now before the situation gets any worse and the humans start asking even more questions."

The leopard shifter ran off to start rounding up the survivors. Jessica would be able to transport them away from public view, hopefully.

"Wait a second." Ethern grabbed Jessica's arm softly, and she stopped.

"What is it?"

"You're not going to like what I'm about to ask. In fact, I think you're going to hate it and me after I say it."

She furrowed her brow together and looked at him.

"I think you better just spit it out."

"We need to find out how powerful Ciaran is. He's just destroyed a massive building and killed hundreds of people in a matter of seconds. That's not normal magic."

Jessica shook her head. "No, it's dark magic—a very powerful kind, and I'm pretty sure, he'll be capable of so much more. But I don't see what this has to do with me?"

"It has everything to do with you, Jessica. You know

him. You know him intimately. What makes him function, and what are his motives? You are the only person on this planet, at the moment, who's capable of working out what else Ciaran Dunaid is capable of doing. You're the person who knows him the best, and you're the only one with any chance of going up against him."

She shook her head.

"No, please don't make me, Ethern. I can't do it."

Ethern took both her hands in his.

"Please, Jessica, look around us at the chaos and destruction, and the faces of terror on the humans. They've just been shown a powerful dark magic that destroyed a building with little effort. Listen to the sirens going off everywhere. This is panic. This is the war. The time for sanctions and talking is over. Actions are now required to protect us and our way of life."

He looked to where a young woman carried her daughter in her arms. He sensed they were both human, and the fear coming from them was overwhelming. The mother had witnessed the end of the world as she knew it and was faced with an alternative reality. On both sides, truths were coming out. Fear would take over soon, and the governments of the humans would seek to destroy the supernaturals because they wouldn't be able to risk considering anything else. The mother was worried about her daughter and thought they would die. Humans believed death was an end to everything, and the worst thing that could happen to them. They didn't know of the possibilities it could bring for rebirth and a different, better future.

The woman disappeared into her house, and using his superior hearing, Ethern heard her place her child down and start to push furniture against her front door as a barricade. It wouldn't protect her if Ciaran came for her, though…nothing would. The only person who stood a remote chance of stopping the druid now was Jessica, but Ciaran was the one who'd broken her in the past.

"Please, Jessica, tell me what you know. Help me. Help your friends." An icy chill ran over him with the realization that Selene's time was coming—the reason she'd been brought to this earth. "Prophecies are everything in our world. Ultimately, a sacrifice will have to be made to save the supernatural world, but I don't want to make it yet, not if there is another way. Jessica, you are that way, please. I'm not asking you to take Ciaran on. All I need is information. Please."

Jessica shook her head again and pulled away from him.

"I can't. I can't do it. I'm sorry."

She melted into the crowd to complete the task he'd given her.

Ethern took one last look at the chaos going on

around him before finding a quiet place to change back into his ant form, and having shifted, he returned to the building to clear up as much damage as he could. It was futile, though. People were about to die, thousands... millions maybe, unless he could get Jessica to change her mind.

CHAPTER SEVEN

*J*essica had almost fainted when she'd seen Ethern was alive. She couldn't believe how he'd managed to escape from the devastation all around them, but he had, and she was grateful for it. Well, she was until he told her he needed her help to bring down Ciaran. It wasn't something she thought she could do. She didn't want anything to do with her former lover. He'd broken her heart when he'd told her he'd been using her. It had shaped a great deal of her life since then and would continue to do so in the future.

She was scared, but at the moment, she couldn't think about that. There was a more urgent need, which was to help those who had survived the destruction of the Reichstag. In total, she'd managed to rescue about fifty people—most were administration staff, not Council leaders. She'd taken them back to the Glacial Blood mansion where Kas had set them up in the cabins, and she'd placed a magical protection enchantment around them. None of the survivors were senior members except Ethern, so it was unlikely Nuka would come after them, but they needed to be careful, just in case.

When everyone was settled and fed, Jessica collapsed in the lounge of the main mansion. It was unusually quiet. All the other pack members were either busy elsewhere or resting after the stressful day. The television was on, but she reached out and turned it off, not wanting to listen to any more about the world going into meltdown because of Ciaran's actions.

Why hadn't she seen what he was like all those years ago?

She was foolish to think he was in love with her. She was even more stupid to have fallen in love with him. When she did learn the truth, she should have put a stop to his plans then and there and not run away. The darkness was always in him. She saw it but did nothing about it. She felt a failure. This was all her fault.

She put her head in her hands and allowed the first tears of sorrow and exhaustion to fall. He'd been a perfect lover to her. *Why did fate hate her this way?* She knew she had feelings growing for Ethern, but she'd never be able to act on them. She was too scared. The multi-shifter had magical powers. What if the darkness claimed him as well? What if it was her who turned men dark? She knew she was just being stupid now, but it was genuinely what she feared.

"You want to talk about it?" The deep timbered voice of her alpha, Kas, filled the room. She hadn't heard him come in, but he stood in front of her with a look of concern on his face. "I've been told I'm a good listener."

Jessica sniffed up her tears.

"I think you'll find you're one of the best listeners here."

"Talk then." Kas took a seat next to her on a battered, old leather couch.

"I'm just tired. Today has been stressful."

"It has." Kas looked mindlessly toward the television. The screen was black, but they both knew what it would show if it were turned on. "That isn't why you're crying, though."

"I'm that obvious?" she questioned.

"I've been an alpha for a long time now. I recognize many signs."

Kas was always more insightful than the rest of the pack.

"It's Ethern," she blurted out.

"Tell me," Kas urged.

"He wants me to work with him to figure out how powerful Ciaran is?"

"And the problem with that is?" Kas shrugged his shoulders.

"I don't think I can. It would mean facing things I've long since buried in the past."

"Buried, but not dealt with."

"I don't need to deal with them. Ciaran cheated on me. He broke me for all future men—end of story." She folded her arms across her chest.

"No it isn't. It's far from the end of the story. You don't trust men. You've decided we're all the same."

"I trust you," she interrupted Kas impatiently. "I trust the rest of the guys in the Glacial Blood pack."

Kas sat back in his seat, his legs crossed at the ankles, and he placed his hands in his lap. It was his thoughtful pose. She knew it well.

"You trust them as friends, as a family, but Ethern, he's different. I'm not blind, Jessica. I've seen the growing bond between you both, and I knew once the others paired up you wouldn't be too far behind them. Don't allow what Ciaran did to you to destroy your chance of happiness. Ethern is a good man—one of the best. I trust him with the lives of everyone in this pack. He's fighting for our future and won't stop until we're safe."

"I'm scared, Kas. I know he's not telling me every-thing. I sense it. He's even hinted at it."

Jessica reached out and grasped Kas' hand with her own for comfort.

"Ethern has been trusted with a lot of information. His mind must be full of all he has to protect. It's an impossible position for him to be in. The weight of our future is in his hands. He's not lying to you. He's doing what he thinks is best to protect you...to protect all of us, and he has my trust. I know he's a good man," Kas reassured her as he pulled her closer to him and tucked her under his arm. She welcomed the comfort from the big polar bear shifter.

"I will help Ethern with Ciaran. It's going to hurt, but it's the right thing to do for the shifters and other supernatural beings. I trust him with the future, but I don't know whether I'll ever be able to trust him with my heart, even though when he's near me, my entire body is screaming out for me to try."

Kas stroked the top of her head. "I sometimes forget you don't have the same understanding of certain things as we do. Shifters are taught to always listen to their bodies from a young age. It's important in order to allow the change to happen. You've not had that teaching. Sometimes you have to allow your body to take over, and rather than hide away from it, you need to hear what it's telling you. Sometimes your body knows best." Kas paused and let out a long sigh.

She felt its warmth pass over her head. The polar bear had become like a brother to her. She adored him and listened carefully to his words. She knew they'd be beneficial for her.

Kas continued, "Not all men are cheaters. There are good ones out there in the world. It might be hard to believe after being hurt so badly, but some men would never hurt another person in that way. I know those feelings only too well. It's the reason I'll never marry."

Jessica looked up at her friend.

"I don't understand?"

"I've been in love, Jessica, but I couldn't allow the love to flourish, because it would have hurt someone close to me. Ethern is a good man. I see it, and I feel it. He won't hurt you. Listen to your heart for once and find the person who'll make you want to get out of bed every day and dance with happiness. It'll be scary taking the risk, but I think you'll find it will be worth it."

Jessica nodded. It was time to stop being scared. A future with Ethern might only be short if they weren't able to save themselves from the war with the humans. She had to try before it was too late.

"I'll talk to him."

"Don't leave it too long." Kas cupped her cheek in a

tender gesture. "Regret is something you can never banish."

The door to the lounge opened. Brayden and his mother, Jane, stood there. Jane looked to where Kas held Jessica's cheeks, and the witch thought she saw a look of sorrow flit through Jane's eyes. She dismissed it when Kas gently moved her away from him so he could stand.

"Is everything all right?" Kas asked.

Brayden looked tired. Worry lines marred his forehead. The beta of the pack was due to become a father any day now, and this was the last thing he needed.

"It's cool. I just wanted to let you know we've got everyone settled. Ethern is still bringing artifacts back from the Reichstag, and I was going to help him catalog them, but Teagan took the task on instead. If it's all right with you, would you mind if I go and check on Selene?"

"No, go be with her," Kas urged

"Thank you." Brayden nodded before he left the room.

"Jane, you need to rest as well. I think we'll have a lot of mouths to feed over the next few days," Kas ordered.

Jane looked tired, and Kas went over to her and took her hand in his. Together they headed out of the door, but as they left, the polar bear shifter turned back to where Jessica was still sitting.

"Don't leave this world with any regrets, Jessica. Go find Ethern," he said with a sorrowful expression.

She nodded.

CHAPTER EIGHT

"Is Jessica all right?" Selene asked, looking up as her husband entered the bedroom followed by Kas and Jane, her mother-in-law.

"What's happened?" Jane questioned with concern.

"Nothing to worry about, just another member of the pack possibly losing their heart." Kas smiled.

"To whom?" Selene was definitely intrigued now.

"I think it's best if she tells you herself." Kas wiped his hands over his face and yawned. "While things are quiet, I'm going to get a few hours sleep. Call me if you need me."

Brayden nodded at his alpha. Selene held her hand out to her husband, inviting him to come and sit with her. He did and placed his hand on her growing belly. It instantly started to vibrate in a purr as the child within her sensed its father's calming presence.

"How are you feeling, Selene?" Jane remained standing by the door.

"Tired more than anything. I know the time is coming. I can feel the baby moving around and getting ready to be born. I'm nervous, especially with what happened today. Will we be able to control his powers? I don't want to ask Jessica to bind them, but I think we might have to."

Selene felt tears prick in her eyes. She'd been thinking of nothing but the future of her child since she'd first heard about the events at the Reichstag. A symbol of hope for the shifters had been laid to waste, and with its destruction came the worry of their discovery.

"We'll keep our child protected, don't worry. I won't let anything happen to either of you." Brayden kissed her on the cheek and then moved to kiss her stomach as well. The baby inside her let out a little kick of excitement, and Selene rubbed the spot where she'd felt the movement.

"Would it be better going back to Death Valley?" Jane pondered.

"I don't think so. We're safer all together here," Brayden answered before Selene could respond.

She was grateful for his answer, though. The last

place she wanted to be heavily pregnant was in one of the hottest places in the world, but if it meant safety for her child, she would go there.

"I was wondering about going to the multi-shifters' cave after the birth. Maybe I'll be able to find out more information there about our little one."

"I'm coming with you if you do," Brayden immediately insisted.

"You'll be needed here. I can't believe what Ciaran did. It's terrifying. Thinking about all those people who lost a loved one today is heartbreaking…so many families." This time, the tears started to fall. Selene couldn't help it. She was a hormonal mess. "The world is falling apart around us. With the child of our love about to be born, this should be the happiest time of our lives, but instead, I'm worrying over everything. I don't know what to do."

Brayden pulled her closer while Jane knelt down in front of her. Since Brayden's mother had found Selene wandering aimlessly through the Nevada desert, Jane had become like a mother to her. Selene had been reborn as a multi-shifter with no idea of who or what she was, and Jane had taken her in and helped her discover so many truths.

"I promise you. We'll make the world a better place for my grandchild. I won't let your baby suffer," Jane reassured her.

"I know," Selene replied with a loud sob. "Damn hormones."

Jane chuckled. "I suffered badly as well. Heath was always saying I was either up or down, depending on which way the wind was blowing. It was funny when I look back at it, but I didn't have the pressure you do. Kas will make sure to protect you, and Brayden is just like his father was—he'll lay his life down for his offspring." This time, it was Jane's turn to become tearful.

"Mom, please. I know there's more to my dad's death than you're telling me. Please, before it's too late. I have to know."

"No." Jane stood up and started to walk toward the bedroom door, her shoes clicking on the wooden floor.

"Mom, please."

Brayden was up on his feet and grabbed hold of his mother's arm. Selene sat quietly and watched. She knew as well as Brayden there were a lot of secrets around the death of his father, Heath. She didn't understand why there was the need for secrecy, but she supported Brayden whenever he worried about it or felt the need to try to discover what happened. It was important to them both. Selene knew deep down, though, Jane would tell them only when the time was right.

"No." Jane turned to face her son. "I can't, Brayden.

The time's not right. You need to be strong right now, and this is something you can't be worrying about. It's in the past. Selene and the baby she's carrying are the future. You need to be focused on your family and the pack, making sure they're supported and ready for what might be coming in the next few days, whether it's from the humans or Nuka and Ciaran. You have to understand Brayden, knowing the truth will only hinder you. It won't help. All you need to know is that your father loved you. Just keep that in your heart."

Selene felt her baby kick beneath her hand. It was listening to the conversation. The infant knew its father and grandmother were in distress and didn't like it. She stroked at her rotund belly.

"It'll be all right," she whispered in a calming tone.

Jane looked over to her, understanding what Selene was feeling because she'd experienced the same emotions when carrying Brayden.

"I don't know if I can do that, Mom. It's clawing away inside me. I imagine different things. Was it painful for him? Did he suffer badly? You've kept every-thing from me."

Even though he was almost twice the size of her now, Jane wrapped her arms around her son and pulled him close to her.

"He died knowing he was loved and was surrounded by people who cared for him. I've carried his memory with me ever since that day, and so will you. You'll be the leader of this pack one day and the man you were destined to be."

Jane looked over at her daughter-in-law. They all knew Selene was fated to play a large part in the war ahead. No one knew exactly what it was except it would be pivotal.

"We need to focus on being a family and protecting the baby when it comes. There's no point in dwelling on the past. Let's look to the future."

Brayden pulled back from his mom. "The future? How can we look forward to a future that will probably mean our captivity? What type of life is that for my child?"

Selene could feel her husband's anger rising. She placed her hands over the child in her stomach, giving it as much comfort as she could.

"The world as we know it is falling apart. People will die—shifters, humans, other supernaturals. All because of the whim of a mad man who I know is responsible for my father's death, even if you won't tell me."

"Nuka Lincoln didn't kill your father," Jane instantly spits out.

"Why do you insist on protecting him?" Brayden threw his hands up in the air. "I give up. I'm not going to sit by and watch this happen anymore. I'm going to put an end to it."

Brayden pushed past his mother as Selene watched on in alarm.

"Brayden," she called after him, but he was already out of the door and starting to shift.

"Brayden," Jane called as well.

In the next second, there was a flash in the room, and Brayden in snow leopard form had returned. His body immediately transformed back to human.

"No!" he shouted furiously.

Selene's body had turned green with Wiccan tattoos. Brayden shifted and again made a run for the door but was immediately brought back. The baby was controlling Selene's body in order to stop its father from doing something stupid.

"Stop it," Brayden shouted loudly, the sound echoing around the room.

He started for the door again, but it was slammed shut in his face before he could reach it by his unborn infant.

"Brayden, listen to your child," Jane pleaded.

Selene took back control of her powers, and sliding from the bed, she went over to her husband who stood defeated by the door. She looked at Jane, who nodded, and with a flick of her wrist, Selene transported Brayden's mother from the room to her own bedroom.

"I'm going to have a major talk with that baby when it comes out. I'm the boss, not him or her," Brayden complained.

Selene let out a wry laugh.

"I think from the moment it was conceived, it took charge of us." She looked down at her stomach. "I'm scared, Brayden."

He pulled her to him and kissed her lips.

"So am I," he replied, and it calmed her to know she wasn't alone with her fears.

"Take me to bed, husband. Remind me of the love in this world."

He leaned forward and rested his forehead against hers.

"As long as we're together and fighting, there'll always be love."

CHAPTER NINE

The elation Nuka felt as he watched Ciaran bring down the Reichstag building had been overwhelming. It had brought about the end of the shifter's Council. The Council leaders who'd kept them hidden away from humans for so long were no more. Only a few stragglers remained, and none of them would be able to mount any defense against his power and what was coming.

Nuka sat in an old, wingback, leather chair placed at the edge of Ciaran's magic room. His grandfather was sat in the middle of the room within a pentagram. Ciaran had placed the five-pointed stars everywhere around the house to feed his power. He was an exceptionally powerful druid now, but he was also loyal. He knew the value of Nuka's plans for world domination. Together they were the best team.

"Is this going to hurt?" his grandfather protested.

"Everything good hurts, Mr. Lincoln," Ciaran replied and painted a black line of ink down his grandfather's forehead.

"It'll be quick," Nuka added. "And then we can run together."

"My bear is angry. He's not sharing well with Samuel," his grandfather complained.

At the start, the only way to bring Nuka's grandfather back to life was to combine his body with Samuel's. Both men needed to be separated now, and with Ciaran's newfound magical abilities, it was possible.

"What will happen to Samuel?" Nuka questioned, picking up the glass of brandy from the table next to him.

He took a sip of the fiery liquid and placed it back down. He wasn't in the mood for drinking a lot tonight. His own polar bear was itching to come to the surface to roam free and hunt for seals.

"Samuel died when we resurrected your grandfather," Ciaran explained while he continued to place herbs and various symbols on the floor within the pentagram. "He'll come back as a demon. It'll be interesting to see if he has any powers in his new form."

Ciaran pointed to some symbols within the pentagram. "I'm writing a few useful abilities down, and fate will choose which, if any, he possesses." The druid moved his fingers across the patterns on the floor—fire, teleportation, ice. "I've chosen ones that will benefit us the most."

"Let's hope fate chooses wisely." Nuka acknowledged the symbols. "And cleans up after itself. When this war is over, I'm going to have to redecorate this place."

"You mean you'll still be living here?" Ciaran questioned in surprise.

"True. I've always fancied a British Palace as my summer home and the White House as my base for business. Both of those would need a thorough makeover as well, though. Too old-fashioned and boring for my taste. So many rooms and not enough whores in them."

"I don't know?" Ciaran chuckled, and Nuka joined in.

"Come on, let's get on with this. We set the plan in motion at the Reichstag today. I want the reverberations of this to hit all around the magical world tonight. I want them fearing for their lives. I want them brought to their knees, begging for us to help them because it's the only way. After that, you'll destroy the humans, burn them alive, send them a plague of suffering. I don't care how you do it—I just want every last one of them gone, so we can rule this world as gods."

"I like the sound of that," Ciaran agreed.

The druid shut his eyes, and when he opened them again, Nuka noticed they'd turned black. The spell was underway. Words he didn't understand came from Ciaran's mouth. They filled the room with a powerful aura. Black smoke rose from the wooden floor, or maybe from even deeper below. *From hell itself?* Nuka wasn't sure where Ciaran drew his powers from ultimately, but he had a good idea they weren't from heaven. All the black was a big clue.

Nuka crossed one leg over the other and watched intently as the smoke wound its way into his grandfather's body through his nose and ears. His grandfather started to scream in pain like Ciaran said would happen. Nuka didn't flinch or make any movement to help his older relative. No, this was necessary to achieve what they all wanted, so he simply sat still and watched.

Another sip of brandy passed the time while Ciaran continued to recite the magical rhyming words, and the black smoke cocooned his grandfather until all that was visible was the top of his head, and eventually, that disappeared as well. Things were about to get interesting. He placed the brandy back down and leaned forward in his seat. His polar bear itched to come out, but he tampered it down.

Soon.

Very soon.

The bear remembered his youth—the times he ran with his grandfather's bear, and the times they'd hunted together. Nuka's grandfather was more like a proud parent to him than his own father had been. Until his death, his father had always spent his time with Kas. Nuka's twin had never enjoyed the kill. He never tortured his prey before killing it and eating it raw like Nuka did. Kas killed instantly. He never made his food suffer. He was a wimp.

The wrong brother had been born first, and as a consequence, shifters had been forced to remain in the shadows, living in fear of exposing their true natures. Too many years of Nuka's life had been wasted realizing this and putting plans into place to stop it. Why should shifters hide? Why should they pretend not to be wild animals, just because of human sensibilities? It was a complete crock of fucking shit, decided by a few men in suits at the Council.

Well, they were all dead now. It was their punishment for making shifters hide their abilities. Soon he would walk through one of the world's biggest cities in animal form—a city that was a symbol of hope for so many, and he would destroy it with his grandfather,

Ciaran, and Samuel by his side. He couldn't wait. He could almost taste the victory on his lips. It would be sweet as honey.

He was brought out of his reflection when he was pushed backward on his chair across the floor as a powerful blast of energy ripped through the room. The walls shook, the windows were blown out, and the bottles of various herbs and tonics were smashed. At the same time, the candles illuminating the vast majority of the room, except for a small electric lamp on Ciaran's desk, were also extinguished.

Looking up, Nuka was elated with what he saw. The black shadowy cocoon in the pentagram had disintegrated leaving him with the view of his grandfather and Samuel standing together, side by side. Ciaran turned a complete circle in the center of the room with his hands outstretched, and any damage he'd caused was immediately repaired. His black eyes changed back to normal, and the druid looked smugly on at the results of his hard work.

"Samuel?" Nuka questioned as he rose from his chair and approached the ex-councilman who was staring straight ahead.

Samuel didn't look any different from the last time Nuka had seen him earlier that same day. While sharing a body, his grandfather and Samuel had circled around who had control of it. Nuka had got used to seeing his grandfather's face one moment and then Samuel's the next.

"Great power. I feel it everywhere within me." Samuel finally spoke. He held up his left hand, midway in the air. "I'm different."

"You're dead," Ciaran reminded him.

Nuka waved his hand to quieten the druid. "Allow the power to envelop you. Give you your true form."

They all looked at Samuel's raised hand. Sparks were emerging from the tips of his fingers—they ignited into large flames that spread up Samuel's arm and over his back and front. In no time at all, Samuel's human form was fully ablaze and gave off a tremendous heat. Stepping back, Nuka guided his grandfather to the chair he himself had recently vacated. The elderly man was disorientated. It appeared he'd not yet fully returned to his body.

Ciaran held his hand up and formed an icy barrier around Samuel as the man continued to burn but made no sounds of pain. Eventually, the flames subsided, and Ciaran removed the ice. In place of Samuel's human form was a demon—a fire creature with red skin charred black in patches.

"I like this." Samuel shot sparks of fire from his fingers and relit every candle in the room. "It's a power I'm going to enjoy using. Anyone for a human BBQ session?"

Nuka laughed. "Soon my friend." He turned his attention back to Ciaran. "You must have pleased whoever controls the bestowing of powers. That's the best power we could have asked for. It's going to cause an incredible level of destruction."

"It's perfect," Nuka's grandfather gasped next to him, finally landing back in his body.

"Are you all right?" Nuka questioned.

"Fuck me, you weren't kidding when you said it was painful," his grandfather complained and wagged an accusatory finger at Ciaran.

"I'm sorry, Mr. Lincoln." Ciaran bowed his head in respect. "How do you feel?"

"Good."

It was Nuka's grandfather's turn to hold his hand out. They all watched intently as the four fingers and thumb changed into the paw of a polar bear. Nuka's bear roared inside him as his grandfather transformed into the polar bear he remembered from his youth.

"Ciaran, Samuel, prepare for the next stage in our plan. We attack tomorrow. Tonight, though, I'm going to run with my grandfather."

CHAPTER TEN

The sharp pain ripped through Jessica's head like someone was stabbing a knife into the top of it. She pushed herself from the bed and fell on the floor. The blinding pain was getting worse. A scream sounded from somewhere else in the house… Selene. Jessica gasped as black smoke swirled around her and captured her in its presence.

"Help!" She faintly heard Brayden shouting from outside.

She let out a loud scream of her own, and her bedroom door burst open. She could just about make out the shadowy figures of Kas and Zain in the doorway.

"Shit," one of them exclaimed.

They tried to enter the room to get near her, but the

black smoke prevented them from doing so. It pushed them away as the pounding in her head continued. She screamed again, and the sound was echoed back from Selene and Brayden's bedroom.

"What the hell is going on?" Someone tried to get near her again.

"Ciaran," another replied, his voice full of worry.

The pain was spreading down Jessica's body. It felt as though her insides were being ripped out, and all the magic within her was circling hard and surging away with the black smoke, except it wasn't—it was still there. It had to be Ciaran doing this. He was using the collective magic existing in the world to perform a spell that was sure to have devastating consequences. The pain was becoming unbearable. She tried to think of words, spells, anything that would help her to get rid of the agony, but there was nothing in her memory. It was empty except for the pain. She struggled to breathe as she heard the shouts of anguish from the rest of the Glacial Blood pack surrounding her.

"How do we stop it?"

"We can't."

"God help them."

Jessica's eyes clouded over. Blinded to everything around her, she felt before she saw the polar bear running free in front of her, followed by a strange crea-ture with red and black patches covering its body. She reached out to try to touch them but couldn't. Her vision returned in a flash as the black smoke encasing her disintegrated with a tremendous explosion in the room. The whole building vibrated, and the pain immediately stopped. She slumped to the floor gasping for air.

"Jessica?" Kas was with her, holding her and searching her eyes for signs of recovery.

She was breathing hard, struggling to get air into her lungs.

"Ciaran," she managed to get the name out.

A second later, the room filled with energy, and Ethern appeared in only his underwear. He was in exactly the same state as her, gasping for breath and holding his head as he collapsed on the floor beside her.

"Ethern!" Isobel exclaimed and ran to check on him.

Jessica turned her head to look at the multi-shifter. His body was in the form of a witch, and his eyes were wide with fear. He tried to mouth something to her but couldn't get the words out.

"Get them water," Kas ordered, and a few seconds later, she was sat up and droplets of water were being placed at her lips. "Breathe," Kas ordered, "with me."

Jessica watched her alpha as his chest rose and fell. She copied the action, and eventually, her breathing started to level out. Zain and Isobel were doing the same with Ethern who'd now turned back to his human form. Once Jessica's breathing had returned to normal again, she collapsed back down onto the floor.

"What happened?" Kas asked.

"A spell," Jessica responded as her polar bear alpha put another couple of drops of water to her lips. "Ciaran...I think he's done something bad."

Zain stood up from where he'd been sitting with Ethern who was now propped up against the wall, and Isobel was helping him drink.

"I'll go and check the latest news." The bear shifter offered.

As Zain left, Selene appeared at the door, assisted by Brayden and Jackson, the black panther shifter who'd recently joined the pack. He'd left Nuka's pack after realizing the polar bear had been keeping him under a spell for years. Katia, a shifter tigress and Jackson's other half, was there as well.

"It was so powerful!" Selene exclaimed as she was helped to a seat by Brayden and Jackson. "I've never felt anything like it, even when he was given the dark powers."

"I haven't either," Ethern added.

Kas assisted Jessica to stand and walked her over to her bed.

"His power is growing." Jessica had sensed it from the very start of whatever had just happened to them. The pain they'd suffered had come from its increasing strength. "And now, he's drawing on our powers to do his spells."

Selene's eyes went wide, and she covered her belly with her hands. "Is my baby safe?"

Jessica pushed off the bed. Her legs were wobbly, and Kas helped her to go to Selene. The witch placed her hands on Selene's belly and allowed her mind to go blank. They hadn't been using ultrasound to check on the unborn infant. Jessica had connected with the magical side of the baby and made sure everything was all right that way.

"Fine, sleeping actually." Jessica let out a chuckle.

It was probably the only time the infant would ever sleep through anything for its parents.

"Thank you." Selene's body turned back to her human form, and Brayden brought his wife closer to him.

"We have to stop him from doing this?" Ethern was finding his voice again. "I feel exhausted."

"I do as well." Selene leaned against her husband.

"We'll start researching in the morning." Jessica announced.

She knew she couldn't hide away from Ciaran any longer. She had to discover what was behind his magic and find a way to bind it before the entire world fell into complete chaos. She'd spent a large proportion of the previous evening trying to avoid the news on the television. But in the short bit she did see, every channel was showing video of Ciaran bringing down the Reichstag, followed by the human leaders discussing what the world needed to do about it.

"Thank you, Jackson." It was Ethern's turn to get to his feet with the panther shifter's help.

Zain ran back into the room. "There's nothing on the television. Either it's not gone live yet, or it was a spell he did in private. What do you think?"

Jessica motioned for Kas to help her back to the bed. He did so and remained standing beside her.

"It must have something to do with the polar bear and the weird red and black demon," she informed them, and they all looked at her like she'd gone insane.

"The what?" Ethern questioned.

"During the spell? Didn't you see them?"

Ethern shook his head. Jessica looked at Selene.

"I'm sorry, Jessica. I didn't see them either."

Jessica felt her breath catching again. If Selene and Ethern had the same experience as her, why hadn't they seen them as well?

"When your vision blurred, did you see anything in the darkness?"

They both shook their heads.

"My vision didn't blur. Ok, with pain, it did, but nothing else. I could see everything around me the entire time." Ethern's brow furrowed.

"The same with me, I focused on Brayden, trying to stop the pain," Selene confirmed.

"Then somehow I was drawn farther into the spell than you both were. There was a polar bear." She looked at Kas. "Just like you. It was there in front of me. I saw it."

"What about the other creature, the demon?" Ethern came closer to her as Kas took a step back. "What did he look like?"

Jessica rubbed at her temples, trying to remember the face, the markings, or anything that could tell her who or what the creature was. An image of its face formed in her mind, and she let out a scared squeal.

"Samuel. It was him. The man who became your grandfather, Kas."

Understanding hit the room, and everyone fell silent at the same time.

"He's managed to separate them." Ethern broke the silence. "A spell no one has accomplished before, but Ciaran promised to perform."

It was Kas' turn to take a stumble backward. "He's becoming too powerful to stop. These spells are not natural. He's exploiting the dark side."

Tears formed in Jessica's eyes.

"Why do I see it? Why am I the only one?" She was terrified.

"I suspect Ciaran made you see it. He's toying with

you because he knows what a powerful witch you could be. You have to help me stop him, Jessica." Ethern got down on his knees in front of her. "Please." He placed his hands on her lap, and she reached out and put hers on top.

"I think we all need to get some rest," Kas spoke up from the corner of the room. He was as pale as a sheet, shocked by the news his grandfather was back as his own person in the world.

Everyone filed out of the room, leaving Jessica alone with Ethern. He was still on his knees in front of her. He stayed that way for a few moments before getting back up. His skin now changed from his human form back to green with brown tattoos. He was going to leave, teleport away. She didn't want that to happen. She had to be brave for the first time in a very long time.

"Don't leave me, Ethern." The words tumbled from her mouth at the same time as the tears fell down her cheeks. "I'm scared. I don't want to be alone. Please, stay. Hold me." She stood up and rushed over to him.

Ethern changed back into his human form again and held out his hand to her. She took it, and he led her back to the bed and settled her on one side before he went to the other, and climbing in, he pulled her close to him. They settled with her back against his front, and his warm breath on her neck.

"I don't know if I can give you what you want, Ethern."

"You don't have to, I'm not going to pressure you in any way. I'm here because you asked me to stay and give you comfort. It's all we both need at the moment. I'll admit I'm scared as well. To feel so out of control of my own body is not something that sits well with me."

"I shouldn't have been so frightened to stop him before. I knew of his dark side and decided to bury my head in the sand about it, but I can't do it anymore. I need to be brave and figure out a way to end this."

Ethern pulled her closer to him. "You won't be alone, Jessica. I'm going to be with you every step of the way."

"Thank you."

Jessica allowed her eyelids to flutter shut. Being wrapped up in Ethern's warmth comforted her. It gave her fresh hope, and she would use it to destroy the man who'd been manipulating her for far too long.

CHAPTER ELEVEN

*E*thern woke from what had been the best half night of sleep ever. His body was still curled around Jessica, keeping her warm and giving her comfort. However, when his dick started to swell at the thought of sinking deep inside her, he knew he needed to pull away, and the second he moved, she woke with a start.

"It's ok," he reassured her when she sat up and blinked the sleep from her eyes.

"What's happening?"

"I was going to go and get us both a drink," he lied, and she nodded at him.

He allowed his skin to turn green, and he teleported down to the kitchen. Kas was the only one awake after the events late in the night. He was sat at the kitchen table with a cup of steaming coffee in his hand. He wasn't drinking it, though, he was just staring straight ahead.

"Morning," the polar stated with a blank expression when Ethern appeared.

"Morning." Ethern cocked his head toward Kas. "Are you ok?"

"I've been better. My long dead grandfather is alive and causing chaos with my twin brother who's dead set on killing all the humans. Is it too early to put whiskey in my coffee?"

Ethern stopped midway through pouring a coffee for himself and Jessica.

"When you look at life that way, no, go for it."

"It's ok. I'll wait until noon at least. I'm sure my brother will cause more problems by then."

"We'll stop them, and Ciaran's head might just be the one we need to chop off to get the rest of the body to die."

"I hope so." Kas sighed heavily. "Go back and look after Jessica. She needs it more than me at the moment."

Ethern nodded. "We'll speak later."

"Of course."

Kas resumed staring at the wall as Ethern returned to the bedroom. Jessica wasn't in bed any longer. She was emerging from the bathroom with a robe wrapped around her. He placed the coffee down on *his side of the bed*, he liked the way that phrase sounded, and allowed his skin to return to that of a human.

"Are you all right?" Jessica looked at him.

"Kas was in the kitchen. I think everything happening so quickly has hit him hard."

Jessica glanced down at the floor with a sad expression before looking up at Ethern again and saying, "We'll drink these and get started. I have something I want to show you."

"Ok." Ethern picked up his coffee and took a sip while Jessica slid back into the bed and pulled the sheets over her.

She took a mouthful of her coffee and let out a contented hum.

"I needed this. I've still got a massive headache. I can't wait to get Ciaran out of my head permanently."

Ethern leaned back against the wall he was standing near and let out a deep breath. Something had been bothering him about Jessica for a long time. He knew she was scared of relationships because of what had happened with Ciaran, but there was something more to it. He'd always sensed it. He had to know.

"Jessica?"

"Yes?" She looked up from her coffee,

"Why are you really scared of relationships?"

Her face deflated, and her shoulders slumped.

"I knew you'd ask me that one day. Telling you it was because I saw Ciaran cheating on me would never be enough for you. You're far too inquisitive."

"No, I just sense there's more to the story than you're letting on."

Jessica patted the bed next to her. He pushed off the wall and took a seat beside her.

"Ciaran cheated on me with my best friend at school. My only friend at school really. I wasn't popular because I was obsessed with studying magic. It didn't bother me, though, because I spent all my time with Ciaran. He showered me with love and attention. I truly thought we would be together forever. I pictured having children with him, buying our first house together, and decorating the rooms with magic. I imagined our wedding—hidden away from the world so we could be who we truly were. I was in love with him. He had my heart." Jessica placed her coffee down on the bedside table when her hands started to shake. Ethern reached out and held them.

"Tell me everything."

Jessica looked up at him and bit her lip. The memories he was asking her to relive were painful.

"When I discovered them together, Ciaran used his magic to pull me to him. He wrapped me in his powers, so I wasn't able to move. He said things that have haunted me ever since. He told me he was using me, feeding off my magic because he knew I was powerful. He told me he'd never loved me. The entire world I'd created around him was a lie. It broke me, and I've found it hard to trust ever since, especially as I barely made it out of there with my life. He held me so tightly in his magic and told me he was going to feed off the rest of me. I'll never know how I broke away, but I did. I imagined a place I could be free, and my powers brought me here to the Glacial Blood lands. Kas welcomed me, and I've been here ever since, but the walls I built up around me, they've never fallen. I'm terrified of being in that position again. I was naïve, and he played upon that. He used me, and I was lucky to have survived with my powers intact."

Ethern was feeling sick at what he'd heard. Jessica was a powerful being, but she was also kind and gentle. She didn't deserve to be used for her powers.

"I sense you're keeping secrets from me too, Ethern. It's why I can't let myself be with you. I don't want to risk getting broken again."

He pulled her flush against his chest. He was keeping a secret. He'd never admitted it to anyone before, but he knew now was the time to reveal it.

"You're right. I have been keeping something from you. I've kept it from everyone." He allowed his skin to shift to his druid form and used his magic to dress himself and Jessica, and she watched on in confusion. "I want to show you."

He held his hand out to her, and taking it, he teleported her away from the Glacial Blood mansion, away from America, and to a small town on the outskirts of the Yorkshire Dales. He knew it well. It had been his home for many years before he was given the abilities he possessed now. His skin returned to normal, and he led Jessica along the road toward a church.

"Where are we?" She looked up at the sky trying to ascertain the position of the sun.

"England."

"I didn't know you lived here? I thought you were American. You have the accent?"

"I learned it after I was changed."

Understanding hit Jessica. "This is where you lived as a human."

"Yes, this was my home. I was born and grew up in this village. Very few people who knew me then would be alive now. It's changed a lot. I lived here as a farmer until the day I died."

They reached the church, and he guided her to where two graves sat together, side by side. One was adorned with his name, and the other belonged to a woman named 'Elizabeth'.

"Who's Elizabeth?" Jessica questioned, scanning the

grave and finding the answer in the woman's surname. She let go of his hand.

"She was my wife. We grew up together and were childhood sweethearts. We married young and would have stayed all our lives here if we'd had a chance. At the time, I truly believed that was my fate, but something changed all that."

Jessica's face paled, and he could feel anger inside her as well as pain.

"I died in a car accident with my wife beside me. We both took our last breaths together, and our human bodies were buried here. I can only assume she went to heaven because the next thing I knew, I was in the multi-shifter cave, and I was reborn as I am now."

"She died, and you didn't." Jessica took his hand again and held it tightly. "Oh, Ethern, I'm so sorry. I don't know how you coped with that."

"For a long time, I didn't have any memory of her, but I kept getting visions of a woman's face, so eventually, I was told a little of my past life. I came here and found our graves. Most multi-shifters never get to have this. They don't know who they were in their previous life. Selene didn't until I told her. It's believed that not knowing where we come from makes us strong enough to deal with our abilities—they are powerful and can easily become out of control if we let them. Having a past can taint our future."

"But to know you survived and your wife died… they didn't have to take her from you."

"They did, so I could become a multi-shifter. If she'd survived, I would have come back here and would never have left. I've felt guilty every single day since, but her life was a necessary sacrifice for the war ahead. Without me, there wouldn't be a Selene."

Ethern couldn't take his eyes away from the graves. His wife had been a wonderful lady. She was helpful around the village, always baking cakes and taking them to those who needed a bit of comfort. She took care of him him after he came home from a long day in the fields. They were in love, completely and utterly, but she wouldn't have handled the magical world. She was too old-fashioned and feared what she didn't understand. She'd have probably been one of the humans who'd have called for him to be burned as a witch.

"Without you, there wouldn't be a lot of hope either."

"So now you know my secret. It's a big one, and it's why I keep it hidden. I don't want it used against me. I'm sorry. I should have told you sooner."

Jessica knelt down by his grave and placed her hand on the grass there.

"Do you still love her?"

Ethern fell silent. His body buried in the ground

loved Elizabeth, but he was a different man now. The greatest excitement for the man in the grave was a successful harvest—Ethern had grown and learned so much in the intervening years. He wasn't the farmer anymore. He was a multi-shifter, and with that came a new and different love, the one he held for Jessica.

"No, the person who loved Elizabeth died in the car accident with her. My memories of our love are gone. I feel affection for her, but I don't love her. I can't because my heart belongs to another, even if she'll never be able to give me hers in return. I'll protect her and love her from afar, forever if I have to."

Jessica got to her feet and took his hand in hers. In the next instance, they were back in her bedroom at the Glacial Blood mansion. He blinked a few times at the speed of her spell.

"What if she wants to try to give you her heart? What if she's only been guarding it for years because of the fear? The reality is, whether she knew it or not, you had it anyway. She looks for you when she knows you're in a room. She hangs off your every word because you're her equal in so many ways. You're the one who fixed her broken heart, and she wants to give everything a try with you because hiding away is only killing you and her."

"If she wants to do that, then I'll help her all I can.

I'll welcome her into my arms, and I'll hold on to her so tightly I won't ever let go."

With his next breath, Ethern lowered his lips to Jessica's. Having admitted their feelings for each other, the strength of the emotion between them exploded in a passionate kiss.

He pulled away and pressed his fingers to her lips.

"Mine, my heart and soul. My raven."

CHAPTER TWELVE

essica couldn't deny her feelings for Ethern any longer. She wanted him and wasn't going to shy away from it. As he pressed his lips against hers, she welcomed them and embraced the desire that spread through her entire body. It was too early to call it love, but her affection for Ethern was strong.

He pushed her tenderly toward the bed, and she allowed him. They fell back together, their lips still joined. When they parted, Ethern rested his forehead against hers.

"I've had dreams about this moment. Imagining what you'd taste like." He kissed the tip of her nose.

"Then don't stop. Find out if the fantasy is as perfect as you'd imagined. Make me feel something. Please,

Ethern. I'm sick of hiding away and pretending I don't want you. Since the moment you first came to the Glacial Blood mansion to visit Kas, I've not been able to get you out of my head. No matter how much I wanted to suppress my feelings, you've been there always. I wish I'd realized it sooner and not waited until the world is possibly about to end."

"It won't. We'll save it together."

Ethern moved so he could kiss her lips again. He was a big man compared to her, but he didn't put any of his weight onto her. She felt the pleasantness of his form covering her, surrounding her, and enveloping her in his affection. It softened the hard exterior she'd built around herself over the years since walking in on Ciaran cheating on her. Ethern moved his hands over her body, searching out any inch of her flesh he could find. Her skin heated from his touch, and she needed more. She wanted to feel him in her most intimate of places.

"Take me, Ethern. I'm all yours."

He didn't need a second invitation. Ethern pulled her top over her head, and she heard him inhale a deep breath when he saw her gossamer flesh and her small breasts encased in a black, lacy camisole. Slipping his hand expertly under the fabric, he teased the peak of her nipple. It was particularly sensitive, and she moaned lustfully.

"A beautiful sound," Ethern growled, the sound reverberating low in his throat.

He slipped the straps of her camisole off her shoulders and arms and removed it to reveal her bare breasts.

"Please," Jessica whimpered. She wanted more of his touch. Every time he caressed her, it felt like sparks of energy cascaded through her body. She'd forgotten what it was like to be worshiped, and Ciaran had never worshiped her like this. Ethern hadn't touched her most intimate places yet, but already, he'd made her feel better than her ex-lover.

"Stay out of your head." Ethern wrapped his hand around her hair and pulled her face up to meet his. His eyes held hers with a dominant stare, commanding her to obey.

"I'm sorry," she tried to apologize, but he immediately stopped her with a breathtaking kiss to her mouth.

"Don't apologize…just focus on this."

Ethern reached under the waistband of the leggings she was wearing. His warm touch against her soft flesh had her concentrating only on him—his handsome face and intoxicating eyes. He lowered her leggings, leaving her naked before him. He took in every inch of her as he pressed tender kisses to her flesh, and she heated to her very core.

"Ethern," she moaned over and over again as he worshiped every inch of her body without actually touching her between her thighs. "Please," she whimpered, and he obliged. His tongue tasted the length of her slit and then dived inside her entrance. She arched her back off the bed.

"Please, please, please." She was wanton, but she didn't care.

She needed this. A magical aura started to surround them, her powers taking over as she wrapped them both in a protective cocoon. Ethern looked up from where his tongue now flicked over her clit and two of his fingers scissored inside her pussy, preparing it for him. He was entranced by the beauty of her magic.

His skin turned green, and the magical symbols appeared on his body. His own aura flowed from him and entwined with hers. He winked at her and continued his ministrations to her sex. He flicked his tongue faster over her clit, and she felt the pressure of an orgasm powering through her body. She writhed under his expert technique as he played her body like a violin virtuoso. It was unlike anything she'd ever experienced before.

Their auras danced above them—red and blue mixing together to form a vibrant purple. It was stunning.

When she came down from her orgasm, Ethern

withdrew his fingers from her body, and she lamented the loss of his touch burning through her soul. He stood up and lowered his boxers. Jessica watched and licked her lips. His dick was long and thick, and when it sprang free, it was hard and ready to fuck her. She'd become immune to seeing the other shifters naked, but this was different. She desired Ethern and was excited to see him and his evident lust for her.

He returned to the bed and leaned over her again.

"Are you sure you want to do this, Jessica?"

She reached out and wrapped her hand around his dick. He hissed a breath in as she pumped his large length a couple of times before letting go and laying back on the bed. She parted her legs to give him full view of her sex—she was ready for him. Their auras still mixed above them on the ceiling. She cast her eyes upward before returning her gaze to Ethern.

"Take me, Ethern. Show me love."

He didn't need to hear her say it twice. In a swift movement, he was covering her again, and his cock pressed at the entrance to her core. She braced herself, her hands gripping the sheets. Ethern thrust into her, and she felt the magic inside her swirl again. Their auras danced even faster above them. Ethern pushed all the way into her before stopping. He was breathing fast, his shoulders rising and falling as he tried to control his desire. She was the same—her breaths came in short pants as the feeling of fullness spiraled out from her core. She rotated her hips and Ethern withdrew.

"I don't know now how long I'm going to be able to last. It's been a long time since I was with anyone."

"Elizabeth?" Jessica questioned.

He nodded in reply.

"So you're losing your multi-shifter virginity?" she questioned with a happy smile on her face.

"You could say that." Ethern laughed. "I can't think of anyone else I'd want to give it to."

Jessica wrapped her arms around Ethern's corded neck and pulled him closer to her. He withdrew his cock from her before slamming back in, and she groaned lustfully as he began to set a punishing pace on her body.

Their auras descended from the ceiling, swirling around them before entering their bodies via their noses and ears. The two of them were now combined physically and magically inside each other. This was more than sex, this was a spiritual connection through their witchcraft. Each time Ethern filled her, Jessica felt like she was flying on a different plane. Every nerve ending in her body tingled with delight. When he pulled out, she landed for a second, allowing the pleasure to build inside her once again for the next time Ethern entered her.

They seemed suspended like this for an eternity—a

ball of pleasure held together with magic and flesh. Eventually her orgasm hit her, and the world exploded around them, sending an ecstasy rushing through her body she'd never felt before. Flowers descended from the ceiling. Rose petals of all different colors scattered around them—their magic was controlling itself now.

Ethern buried himself inside her and roared his release with the ferocity of a lion. She felt it coat her insides, and it set off another release within her. This time, a chorus of angels could be heard around them, singing a heavenly tune to the most beautiful music she'd ever heard. She'd no idea sex could be this wonderful.

Ethern withdrew from her and pulled her into his arms. Both lay there silently, their chests heaving with exhaustion as the rose petals melted into the bed covers and the wooden floor. The music dissipated into the ether, and their auras separated and returned, untangled, to whichever body they originated from.

"Thank you," Jessica whispered.

"Thank you," Ethern returned and pressed a kiss to the tip of her nose.

She snuggled up closer to him and allowed her eyelids to flutter shut. A sudden exhaustion hit her. They needed to get up and start researching ways of stopping Ciaran, but for a few moments more, she wanted to enjoy the safety of Ethern's arms, and the feeling of love coming from him.

What she'd had with Ciaran had been the lust of a schoolgirl. She'd allowed the evil druid to destroy her, but from the moment she'd first met Ethern, he'd been repairing her soul. With him by her side, she could be the witch she needed to be.

"Fuck sake," Kas yelled from outside her bedroom. "All anyone ever does around here is have sex. I thought the shifters were loud enough, but they've got nothing on witches. Bloody angels singing and orchestras!"

Ethern and Jessica's tiredness immediately left them. They broke into a fit of giggles before giving Kas something to really moan about with magical drums playing all around the mansion.

CHAPTER THIRTEEN

*E*thern couldn't stop watching the curve of Jessica's backside as she walked through the hallway of the Glacial Blood mansion and down the stairs to the room where she practiced her magic. The last few hours they'd spent together had been the best of his life.

The love his human form had shared with Elizabeth was different to the love he felt for Jessica as a multi-shifter. He wanted all of this worry to be over so he could spend his time in bed with her, but it wouldn't be possible until they put a stop to Ciaran and Nuka. He knew the surviving members of the Council were safe on Kas' lands, so now he could concentrate on stopping Ciaran before he caused any more damage.

As they passed by the lounge, he could hear the television playing more reports about the previous day's events in Berlin. It frustrated him that he hadn't been able to do anything to prevent it. In truth, he knew he was lucky to have survived the destruction and that was a hard concept for him to come to terms with.

Jessica opened the door for both of them to enter her room. He took a seat on a chair beside a table covered with various herbs used to create potions, and he waited while Jessica went straight to a shelf full of books at the back of the room. He made sure to keep his eyes on her backside the entire time. She was a definite distraction from the chaos going on around them. She pulled a book from the shelf. It was old and bound in a battered, brown leather cover. As she walked back toward him, Jessica clasped the book tightly below her chest so he was able to appreciate the fullness of her breasts while she moved.

"What's that?" he questioned, unable to read a title on the cover.

The elation and happiness that had been written on Jessica's face earlier had disappeared. It was replaced by a look of concern as a line creased her forehead, giving her a deep frown. He cocked his head, silently asking her to explain.

"When I was younger, my family knew of my extraordinary magical ability. It was a gift handed down via the female line, but apparently, none of my ancestors had been as powerful as me. This is the Book of Shadows, and it has been in our family for many generations. It was purportedly given to one of my relatives by a powerful druid who'd miraculously survived the Salem witch trials. It was foretold that one day it would assist a powerful witch to help save the world. None of my family dared open it, or so I thought. The druid gave a warning when he handed over the book. He said, 'Only the most powerful witch will be able to control the magic inside. All others will fail.' "

Ethern watched as Jessica placed the book down on the table. She kept her manicured fingers on it as though she was scared of what it meant to let it leave her possession.

"What do you mean none of your family dared to open it, or so you thought?"

Jessica let out a wry laugh.

"Nice to see you are listening and not just staring at my backside and breasts."

"I'm not a typical man. I'm capable of doing two things at once. It comes with the multi-shifter abilities," he responded and patted the top of his thigh, inviting her to sit in his lap, which she did before continuing her story.

"There is a tale, another one, handed down in my family. It talks of my seven times great-grandmother.

Evidently, she opened the book because she believed the world as she knew it was at risk. It was around the time of the American Revolutionary War."

Ethern nodded. Being born British, he was well aware of the American history during that time.

"She wanted to help the American side and chose a spell from this book to perform. If it worked, it would have left the English incapable of fighting, and the American's would have won the war easily. It wasn't the right thing to do, though. The war wasn't a magical one —it was a human conflict. Man versus man. There was no need for magic to be involved. In spite of her good intentions, the spell backfired and dark magic consumed her. The story tells of how she went insane from the power inside her. Her daughter was able to bind the magic, but my relative killed herself the next day. Her last words were of being surrounded by dark things: demons, devils, and powers that could destroy everything on the planet. She'd witnessed things no good witch ever should."

Ethern had a practical approach to these sorts of stories handed down through the generations. Living in a small village for most of his life, he was used to old wives tales. He wanted to reassure Jessica.

"The story is many years old. I'm sure it's been embellished over time. Maybe the spells in this book are powerful, but they'll not be uncontrollable in the right hands."

Jessica leaned her head against his shoulder.

"I've feared that book all my life and the stories that come with it. I know I'm the one who's destined to open it again. I'm the one who's supposed to perform the spells it contains to stop the world we know from being destroyed, but it terrifies me, Ethern." Jessica got to her feet as she spoke and finally handed him the book. He didn't open it. It wasn't his place. "What if the words on those pages consume me and wrap me up in the dark side of the magical world? What if I become lost to it? I could destroy the world. I'm terrified of this book, but I fear the answers we seek lie within its pages. The only way to stop Ciaran is written in there."

Jessica put her hand over his on top of the book. He felt her fear surge through his body, and from beneath his palm, he could sense the book calling out to her. It screamed at her to open it and save the world. The conflict of two different emotions warring between each other.

"I hear it," he informed her. "The struggle between you and the book. It calls to you, and I don't think you can ignore it any longer. The coming war is different to the one your ancestor found herself facing. This one *is* magical."

He took a deep breath and placed the book back

down on the table. Jessica stood in front of him, head bowed. He got to his feet, and pulling her into his arms, she relaxed into his chest.

"I won't force you to do anything. It's not in my nature. Just know that whatever you choose, I'll be by your side the entire time. I'll be your strength and guidance. I won't let the darkness take you. Trust me."

She looked up and was about to answer him when a loud commotion came from outside the room. The door flew open, and Tyler, the wolf shifter, popped his head inside.

"Jessica, Ethern, you both need to come and see this," Tyler demanded.

"What is it?" Ethern questioned.

Tyler gulped. "Ciaran and Nuka have just landed in New York."

In that moment, Ethern's world fell apart. Berlin had a symbolic place in the shifter's world, but New York was a symbol of hope to the humans. Atrocities beyond belief had been carried out there in the past, and as he raced after Jessica and Tyler into the lounge, he knew more were about to take place.

CHAPTER FOURTEEN

*C*iaran could feel his powerful magic swirl all around him when they landed on Liberty Island in New York. Helicopters appeared from nowhere, Nuka having spread the word that something was about to happen. The journalists inside the aircraft instantly began filming—all vying for top spot on the news headlines. Ciaran was certainly going to give them something big to report on.

The statue shading them from the midday sun was a symbol of freedom and hope for many humans throughout the world, not just in America. It was time to destroy that hope.

"You ready?" Nuka nodded toward him.

A malignant smile adorned the polar bear's face. He loved what was happening. Revealing everything to the world, and making the humans panic. Nuka had a superior sense of smell, and Ciaran was sure the polar bear was thriving on the scent of fear surrounding them.

Ciaran lowered his head in a sign of deference to his alpha before ascending at rapid speed into the air until he was face to face with the Lady Liberty. His eyes turned black, and he reached his hand out and started to summon the copper and iron holding the statue together.

"Stop, move away from the statue," a deep voice sounded from one of the helicopters through a loudspeaker. Ciaran turned to face the Police helicopter and the occupants giving him orders. *Idiots.* "Do it now, hands in the air." *Complete idiots.*

Ciaran turned back to the statue and continued to call to the fibers holding it together. Slowly he pulled them from the place they'd been settled since 1886.

"Stop," the voice called desperately through the speaker again. "We'll shoot."

They warned Ciaran, but he ignored them.

"Fire," the voice called out and a hail of bullets flew at him. They didn't hit him, though. They stopped midair and disintegrated after he flicked his free hand toward them.

"Fire again," the policeman called.

Ciaran rolled his eyes. *Didn't they know he was trying*

to concentrate? He stopped the bullets a second time when they approached. This time, he didn't disintegrate them. He turned them around and fired them back at the helicopter with vengeance. They thudded into the metallic structure but weren't strong enough to down it.

"Fall back," he heard the police officer shout frantically, and the helicopter flew higher into the sky and farther away from him.

The other helicopters filled with journalists also adjusted their positions to increase their distance from him. Ciaran refocused his attention on the statue. Today wasn't about killing anyone, as much as he wanted to. It was about demonstrating what they were capable of doing.

"Stop playing and get on with it," Nuka shouted from the ground with a chuckle.

"Spoilsport, are you sure I can't turn just one helicopter into an inferno? It'll be fun." Ciaran complained down to the ground below where Samuel and Nuka's grandfather also stood.

"Fire is fun," Samuel added and formed a flame in his hand.

"Not yet, that particular piece of entertainment is for when we descend on London and go to Buckingham Palace. Damn Corgi shifters are annoying, and as the public thinks the Queen is human, then killing her will help our cause in more ways than one." Nuka responded with a smirk.

"I can't wait." Ciaran resumed his focus on the statue. He called again to everything holding it together. "Stand back," he warned his associates on the ground while creating a protective barrier around them, to be on the safe side.

The statue shook as Ciaran used his magic to tear it apart. The lady's crown was the first to fall, followed by her flaming torch. Slowly but surely, every part of the statue crumbled to the ground. A silence fell around the gathered onlookers. There were no sounds apart from the helicopters still hovering above—no chatter came from the journalists as they watched their hope disintegrating into the waters of Jersey City harbor.

Ciaran watched on, captivated by the beauty of the destruction. As an American, the Statue of Liberty should have been an icon to him, but instead, it represented a fallacy. Freedom...what a joke. There was no freedom in this world for the supernatural, but that was all about to change.

Lifting Nuka and the others into the air to join him, Ciaran flew them out over New York harbor toward Battery Island, heading for a new destination, and the target for the next part of their plan. Ciaran lowered them, so they were closer to the ground but high enough to pass over yellow taxis traveling through lower Manhattan. The four of them continued on while the helicopters followed at a distance. They passed the Empire State Building in a blur as they flew closer to one of the most densely populated areas of New York, an area where tourists and locals flocked...Times Square.

Ciaran brought them down in the center of the plaza. Most people ran away from them, but a few brave police officers drew their weapons and fired off bullets in their direction. Ciaran destroyed the projectiles without even thinking, such was the extent of his power now.

Nuka stepped to the forefront of the group. Every camera in the location was now focused on the alpha. The large screen at the end of Times Square displayed the image of his face.

"I'm sure you all have one question on your minds at the moment. Why did we just destroy the Statue of Liberty? Well I have a very good reason for doing so. It's represented a falsehood, a lie. Not everyone in this world is free, but we will be soon," Nuka addressed all those watching.

Various armored vehicles appeared, belonging to the police and no doubt the FBI and CIA. All available, highly trained experts would have been called in for this. Men with larger, more powerful guns emerged from the vehicles. Nuka turned his head toward Ciaran,

"Silence them. I don't want my speech interrupted. No killing, though, remember."

Ciaran stepped forward and smirked. "I'm going to need something to vent my blood lust on tonight if you carry on forbidding me from killing anyone."

"Don't worry, I'll find you something." Nuka chuckled.

Ciaran circled his hands together and shot an energy blast out toward the assembled cavalry. It bound them in a ball of energy, preventing them from interrupting Nuka's speech. Several more onlookers started running and screaming, searching for a hiding place, but Ciaran froze them to the spot so they could watch the spectacular show he and his associates were about to put on.

"Thank you," Nuka acknowledged and returned his focus to the sea of cameras trained on them. "As I was saying, freedom in this world is a myth, and humans choose to hide from the truth. Supernaturals are real. We walk among you every day." Nuka removed the suit jacket he was wearing, unfastened the tie from around his neck, and unbuttoned his shirt. "Not just druids, as my friend here has been demonstrating, but animals of all different kinds."

Nuka shut his eyes, and Ciaran watched as his friend transformed into a polar bear and gave a loud growl.

The people around them started screaming as Nuka's grandfather joined his grandson in polar bear form. Both of them roared at the terrified crowd.

Ciaran continued with the next spell. He placed his hand on the top of Nuka's head, and the polar bear's thoughts were immediately projected into the minds of everyone around them and those watching on the television.

"Do you really know who or what the person standing next to you is? Are they human like you, or a shifter like me? Well, I think it's about time we learned."

Ciaran watched the faces of several of the people assembled in the crowd as they realized what was about to happen. They tried to run but were rooted to the spot by Ciaran's magic.

"Ishana ego rota show," the druid started to recite.

It was a wonderful spell, one which twisted the darkness within him and made it dance with joy. Slowly, one by one, anyone who was a shifter in their vicinity started to change into the animal of their birth: tigers, lions, bears, wolves, and wild dogs, dangerous and deadly animals to the humans, appeared beside less deadly ones such as rabbits and deer. It was a strange but beautiful sight. The wildlife of the supernatural brought into the concrete jungle of central New York.

"If any of you think this is a magic trick, be warned it isn't. The animals you see in front of you are real. The person you thought you knew has been hiding a secret because of the fear of retribution, but no more. We're taking back our true forms. We'll no longer hide in the shadows because of your fears." Nuka reared up onto his two back legs and roared loudly. "The animals are taking the world back, and if you don't like it and want to leave…well, we can always do with more fresh meat, so we'll be happy to oblige you with your life choice."

Ciaran clicked his fingers together and everyone who'd been frozen before was freed. The levels of fear in the area were now at epidemic proportions. Many of the humans started running and screaming while others fell to their knees in front of the wild animals among them, pleading for their lives. The shifters were equally agitated—they stank of desperation and prepared to flee as far from the scene as possible. Many were trying to turn back to their human forms, but Ciaran's spell prevented them from doing so until they left New York. On discovering they couldn't transform, the animals chose to run like cowards.

Nuka looked at Ciaran and nodded. The polar bear shifted back into his human form, and his grandfather did the same. Unlike the other shifters present, they could change freely.

"I think we've caused enough chaos for today. Let's go home," Nuka demanded.

"What about a prize to test out my spells on?" Ciaran questioned.

"Bring one of them with you."

Ciaran looked out over the seas of faces before him. The moment he saw the raven haired woman with a look similar to Jessica's, he knew instantly she was the one he'd take. The witch was his nemesis, and he would happily rid the world of anyone who looked like her.

With a click of his fingers, Ciaran placed the three members of his pack and the woman all under his spell and catapulted them back to their home in Canada.

CHAPTER FIFTEEN

Kas couldn't take his eyes off the television screen as the face, so similar to his own, stared back at him and declared war. His twin brother intended on destroying the world they all knew.

He'd never understand why his brother had so much anger inside him. It wasn't necessary. Kas would never have let his brother down. Even now watching the television and the forced changing of shifters in New York city, Kas still missed his younger twin sibling. He yearned for the affection they both had for each other when they were young. It would never return, though. His brother was too far gone. He'd crossed too many lines, and the only way to stop him now was to kill him, but Kas didn't know if he had the strength to do it.

Ever since he'd discovered his grandfather was alive again, he'd been slowly falling apart inside. He wanted to shift, find the highest mountain, and stay there. Hide away from the world in chaos and remain in his polar bear form forever. He couldn't leave his pack, though. They were his family now, and he owed it to them to make them safe again.

The television went black, and Kas broke out of his reflection. All of the other members of the pack had disappeared somewhere and the house was silent. The only person who remained was Jane. She held the television remote in her hand and a lot of concern on her face.

"Talk to me, Kas," Jane urged, placing the remote down on a table filled with various books and magazines along with a couple of baby toys.

She made her way over to him and joined him on the couch. He normally sat in a chair over in the corner of the room when he read, but the view of the television had been better from here.

"What do you want me to say? My brother has just started a war with the humans, and I have no idea how I'm going to firstly, protect my pack, and secondly, stop it."

Jane let out a deep breath of frustration.

"Kas, it's not up to you to save the world. I know you think you should because Nuka is your brother, but it's not your responsibility alone. Looking at what we've just witnessed, I don't even know if it can be saved anymore. The humans are terrified. You saw the looks on their faces, and not all of them will be understanding. You have to focus on your pack and make sure they are safe now. It has to be your priority. There's already suspicion on this house after Lily exposed Selene. The Council managed to make everyone believe it was a computer generated trick, but the Council has gone now. No one will ever be able to sweep under the carpet what Nuka did in New York today. Please don't put such a heavy burden on yourself."

Jane reached out and took his hand, squeezing it with concern.

"It's easier said than done, Jane. I would lay down my life to protect the pack, and I will keep them safe as best as I can, but Nuka is my brother, my flesh and blood. I have to stop him. I can't let him destroy the world we know, even if it means we have to remain hidden in the shadows forever. The human world is not ready for shifters. Nuka has declared war, and it's going to leave so many people on both sides dead. I can't let that happen—if I do, I will be responsible for every single one of those deaths even if you tell me I won't. The solution to all of this is in here." Kas paused and placed his hand on his heart and then his head. "Nuka is a part of me. We were born from the same egg, identical in every way except our souls. I got the lighter side while his half was black and rotten. I should have seen it and put a stop to it a long time ago. I've had the power to do it but not the courage. I do now, though."

At this moment, Kas hated the way he looked because of what his brother was doing. Watching Nuka destroy the iconic symbol of New York city along with the hopes of its people was like watching himself do it. The faces were identical. Emotions surged through Kas' body. He didn't know what was up or down anymore, and he was exhausted from not sleeping. The world was falling apart, and so was he. His entire life had been devoted to his position as alpha of the Glacial Blood pack. He'd had no life as a result, but he'd also been a coward, hiding behind his responsibilities. It was time he made amends.

"Kas." Jane moved her hand to stroke at his chin. "Please don't do this. Don't blame yourself"

"I have to," Kas replied, "because he's my brother."

Tears formed in Jane's eyes. Kas had always held affection for her. There was a time when he…no, he couldn't think about that now. It would distract him from his resolve to destroy Nuka. He couldn't have any ties. This moment in time was the reason for his existence in the world. This was what he was born to do. This was the destiny he'd been told about all his life.

"No, you have to stop thinking you need to do this alone. You have so many people around you who will help."

"And I won't let them. I care too much for them. Nuka has tried to destroy my family far too many times. The members of my pack need peace and quiet and to live their lives with happiness. You deserve it as well. You have the birth of a new life to look forward to soon. Selene is young, and she'll need your help."

"Don't call me Grandma," Jane interrupted him before he could finish what he was saying.

"I won't. I like my balls where they are." Kas tried to lighten the conversation.

"I'm too young to be a grandma. I don't feel old enough, even though I've been a widow for more years than I was married." Getting to her feet, Jane let go of his hand, and it felt cold instantly. "But stop trying to change the conversation. Kas, you have to promise me you won't do anything stupid. Work with Ethern and Jessica, and the surviving members of the Council. Please don't take Nuka on alone. Not with the magic Ciaran now has at his disposal."

Kas got to his own feet.

"I promise," he confirmed, but it was a false assurance.

He couldn't make that promise. He didn't know what he was going to do yet, but he wasn't ruling anything out. He would do whatever was necessary to stop Nuka causing any more damage.

"You always were a terrible liar." Jane shook her head at him and stormed across the room toward the door.

Kas didn't know what came over him. In an instant, he was following her. In the next, he had turned her around and backed her against a wall. His lips pressed against hers in a searing kiss neither of them expected.

Voices sounded from outside, and they pulled apart, just in time, before several of the pack and a couple of the councilmen came into the room. Jane pressed her fingers to her mouth. Kas could still feel the imprint of her lips on his. He'd made a mistake. He shouldn't have done that.

Without another word, Kas turned on his heels and stormed out of the room. As he went, he shifted and raced through the corridors as a polar bear. He didn't care who saw him. He just needed to get away to clear his head. Too many painful memories lay between him and Jane, including a truth Brayden could never know.

CHAPTER SIXTEEN

"I can't believe he did that." Ethern slammed his fist into a wall in Jessica's magic room. "Those poor shifters he exposed—he's ruined their lives. They'll be hunted down and captured. The television news channels will have pictures of them, and the human governments will identify them and use the images as evidence against them. Who does Nuka think he is? I argued in favor of arresting him years ago, but we couldn't, because we couldn't prove he'd done anything wrong at that point."

In another frustrated outburst, Ethern knocked a chair to the floor. Jessica stepped away from him and allowed him to vent his anger. Ethern was normally a completely placid and mild mannered man, so to see him this way was testament to the pain he was suffering.

The Book of Shadows she'd pulled out earlier was still on her table. Jessica placed her hand on it. It was still calling to her, begging her to open it and dive into its spells. She still couldn't do it, though. It terrified her beyond all belief, even if Ethern promised to keep her grounded.

Ethern's rage finally stopped, and he slumped against the wall he'd previously punched.

"How the hell do we end this?" The defeated multi-shifter looked up at her. She'd never seen him so broken before. She shook her head.

"I don't know. I'll keep checking my spells."

Ethern must have seen where she had her hand because he pushed off the wall and in a couple of long strides was beside her, and his hand rested on top of hers over the book.

"Please, Jessica, we have to try."

"I can't." She pulled away from him, taking the book with her and putting it back on the shelf. "You saw what Ciaran was like. What if I become the same? I could do more harm than good by opening that book. If I can't control what's inside it, then it'll consume me."

"I'll be by your side the entire time?" Ethern pleaded and gently pulled her to him. His eyes searched hers, and she felt his desperation deep in her soul.

"I don't think that even works," she replied, shaking her head.

She needed to put some space between them. The feelings she had for Ethern were clouding her judgement. She was terrified of losing him when she'd just found herself opening up to the possibility of love again.

"I'm so tired, Ethern," she said with a sigh. "The world will never be the same again after today. I want to stop it, but I'm terrified of making it worse. Ciaran tried to feed off my magic once before. What if he tries again and succeeds? It would make him stronger. No one will be able to stop him. I can't risk it."

Ethern shut his eyes, a deep frown marred his handsome features.

"I want to show you something." He opened his eyes again, and his skin turned from human to druid. "It was shown to me the day I became a multi-shifter. Apparently, the reason I was given a second chance at life was to prevent what was revealed. Will you let me show you the same thing?"

Jessica moved her mouth, trying to form an answer, but no words would come. She trusted Ethern, and she knew that what he'd show her would be a truth, but at the same time, she wasn't sure she wanted to see it.

"Ok," she eventually managed to respond.

Ethern took her hands in his large ones and placed

them on either side of her head over her temples. He whispered a few unintelligible words. Jessica felt like she was flying through the air. Her head spun, and she shut her eyes so she wouldn't be sick.

"Where are we going?" she questioned.

"The future," Ethern responded, his tone firm but quiet.

"The future?"

Jessica clung tighter to his hands as the sensation of movement stopped. Her eyes were still scrunched tightly shut—she didn't dare open them to see where they'd landed. Time travel wasn't possible, was it? The magic Ethern was using was beyond her comprehension. Surely, if he had abilities like this, then he was perfectly capable of stopping Ciaran on his own?

Seemingly able to read her mind, Ethern dropped their hands from her head and responded to her thoughts,

"We haven't traveled anywhere. In reality, we're still in your magic room. We've stepped into a vision of the future as it stands now. It's an ability multi-shifters possess because of the way we're born. No multi-shifter is born without a good reason, and my destiny was foretold in the visions of those who came before me. Multi-shifters are seers more than anything."

"Explains a lot."

Jessica still hadn't dared to open her eyes. There

were no sounds around her other than a few birds chirping out a morning chorus.

"Jessica, I've got you. But you need to see this for yourself. Please open your eyes."

Slowly she did as Ethern asked and allowed her eyes to adjust to the rays of a dawning sun. She knew instantly where they were—her home in the Glacial Blood lands, and the mansion loomed in front of them. There was no sound, though, apart for the birds. There was no laughter or chatter from any of the pack members. A house normally full of people was silent. When she took a longer look at the mansion, she saw why. The windows were boarded up. 'Do Not Enter' signs had been placed all along a barbed wire fence that looked like it'd been erected in a hurry. The way the leaves were settled around the walls and the dirt covering the building, suggested it hadn't been occupied for a long time.

"How far into the future is this? Where is everyone?" she fired off two quick questions while pushing a torrent of further queries to the side for now.

"We're ten years in the future," Ethern replied, taking her left hand in his and pulling her close to him. "No one can see us, but we can see them. Come, we have to walk."

She followed along beside him, and as they walked, the scenery around them changed. African plains loomed large in front of them now. The land was barren. Nothing grew there, and while she knew drought often preceded the rainy season, the desolation of the vast expanse before them suggested this would never return to a savanna abundant in green grass.

"What happened here?"

"We don't know for certain. We can only see the same as you do now. It looks like the rains stopped or the land was overworked."

Ethern nodded toward where a lion had appeared. His mane was straggly, and he was painfully thin. Alongside him were two younger lions, a male and female.

"Scott?"

Jessica recognized him instantly, in spite of the dramatic change in his appearance. Gone was the once proud lion who spent more time doing his hair in the morning than anyone else in the house. The three lion's shifted into human form, and Jessica winced when she saw Scott's emaciated body. She took a long look at the children. They were in better health, and she suspected it was because Scott was giving them all the food. It hit her who the children were, Morocco and Zahara. Where was Emma?

"Are you all right, Dad?" Morocco bent down to his father when Scott fell to the ground.

"I need to rest," Scott responded through labored breaths.

Zahara sat next to him and stroked his head. Both she and her twin brother looked sorrowfully at each other.

"Why did they send us here? We don't belong here." The little girl's eyes pooled with tears. "We're not monsters."

"Lion's belong in the savanna," Scott gasped for air as he replied.

Morocco joined his sister at their father's side.

"You're going to leave us, aren't you?"

"I don't have a choice. I've done all I can for you. Remember everything I've taught you and look after yourselves." Scott rolled over and collapsed on his side.

"It's just like Mamma all over again." Zahara broke into a fit of sobs.

Jessica was struggling to watch this, but Ethern kept her rooted to the spot.

"Please, Dad. Don't leave us." the young lioness whimpered.

Scott held both his children's hands. His breath had become shallow, and Jessica knew he didn't have much longer left.

"Go find shelter. Don't let the hunters get you. It's the hunting season soon. Head for the farthest point from the human camps and hide." Scott continued to advise his children, "Make sure to stay away from the real lions and their packs. I love you both. I…" Scott let out a long gasp. "I'll tell your mamma you love her. We'll watch over you from heaven."

One more long breath, and her friend fell silent. His chest stopped moving, and Jessica knew Morocco and Zahara were orphans in a world where hunters now targeted shifters.

"I can't watch anymore," Jessica cried as she pulled Ethern away from the tragic scene.

Their surroundings changed again. This time they were in a graveyard.

"Please, no more, Ethern."

She couldn't do this—possibly see more evidence of her friends dying or already dead. She didn't have a choice, though, for in the distance, a lonely figure dressed in black caught her eye. Isobel stood weeping at a grave. Next to her was Jane, and she too was dressed all in dark colors. They were both looking down at the graves in front of them. Jessica didn't need to see the headstones to know whose names were inscribed there.

"Zain, Brayden?" she questioned Ethern, but he didn't respond.

The two human women stepped aside to reveal the headstones and the identities of those buried there. Zain's and Brayden's names were there. But also

Selene's was written beside her husband's along with the name of a little boy, Heath. He'd died when he was two years old, according to the wording.

Jessica swallowed deeply, trying not to allow the vomit to rise in her throat when she read the words written below the names, 'Executed for crimes against humans'. She knew her friends—they'd never have hurt the humans in any way. Their crimes, if any, would only have been against shifters.

Isobel and Jane turned to face her. They couldn't see her, but she could see them. What she saw was possibly even worse than the graves of her friends. Both women had tattoos on their foreheads, labeling them as traitors to the human race for sleeping with shifters.

Before she could say anything or start to fall apart even more, she was pulled away by Ethern and into a clinical, white room.

"Please, can we go back? I don't want to see any more. I can't."

Even Ethern had tears in his eyes.

"I think this is the one you need to see the most." He stumbled over his words, emotion flooding through him.

"Ok, bring them in." A man appeared in scrubs.

He was prepared for surgery. The doors to the room opened, and Kas was marched in, followed by Nuka. Both were in human form and wore collars around their necks, attached to chains. Men jabbed at them with electric cattle prods, especially when Nuka tried to lash out. Neither of them wore clothes, and Jessica could see various scars covering their bodies.

"What happened to them?" she questioned, squeezing Ethern's hand tighter.

"I've watched this a few times, and the only thing I've been able to come up with is they've been experimented on. They've been operated on to try and discover the key to how they shift—maybe to stop them from changing. Nothing has worked, though."

Ethern jerked his head toward Nuka who'd transformed into a polar bear and was currently being sedated by the guards before he could attack anyone. Kas remained silent with his arms by his side, and his face cast downward. The man in scrubs went up to him.

"You're not thinking about changing as well, are you? Give us all a little show. You're brother isn't such a big man now *we* control *him*." Kas didn't say anything. He didn't even look the man in the face. "It was fun, you know, watching him realize he could never escape after I hung his druid and burned the body so he couldn't return."

"Ciaran?" Jessica gasped.

"That druid wasn't so powerful when he was screaming for his life," the man in scrubs continued.

"They killed Ciaran?" Jessica questioned.

"It would appear so," Ethern confirmed and then fell silent.

"You want to tell me how you felt when I killed your witch? Shame I had to do that. She was a pretty one, but government rules are what they are—no magical beings are allowed to live, not that she was very magical. She was too much of a coward. At least, we got to keep shifters. We can control you and make your life hell." The man cackled.

"I've seen enough." Jessica pulled on Ethern's arm. "Please, take me home."

Ethern nodded and placed their hands at her temple again. The world whooshed by, but she barely noticed. She was too wrapped up in what she'd just seen. When they landed back in the real world, away from the vision, Jessica broke down. She hunched over and sobbed for what was about to happen.

Ethern stepped away from her. She suspected he'd seen that vision many times. He'd said it had been one of the first things he'd seen when he was brought back to life. She was sure if she'd been shown that, she'd have killed herself again, then and there. It was a heavy burden to carry. She allowed the emotion to flow from her body in a puddle of tears on the floor. Her eyes hurt and her nose was stuffed from crying. Her heart was heavy with the powerful anger and distress she felt.

"I'm sorry I had to show you that," Ethern finally spoke. "No one should ever have to see it. I wish I could erase the memory of it from my mind, but I can't. We can change what happens. Nothing is ever set in stone. That is the future, at the moment, but it can be changed. If we do nothing, though, then the world we know is over,"

Jessica heard the door open and shut. Ethern had left her alone. He'd walked away from her after showing her the most distressing thing she'd ever seen in her life, but she understood why. What happened next was up to her and her alone. She needed to make the decision and not be guided by anyone else. He'd shown her what he could. He'd given her his love, and she'd fallen for him in return. But now, it was time for her to save the world.

Making her way quickly over to the bookshelf, she retrieved the book given to her by her ancestors. She placed it down on the table in front of her and held her hand over it. Still, even after everything she'd seen, she struggled to open it.

"God damn it," she shouted up into the air. "I'm not weak. This book was meant for me, and I will put a stop to what Nuka and Ciaran are doing. I'll save the world from imploding in on itself. I have to. I'll never be able to live with myself if I don't."

She took a deep inhalation and opened the book. A

great power surged through her—there was darkness but also light. When she looked down at the page open in front of her, it revealed the spell she needed.

'To bind darkness in another Wiccan.'

A strong pair of arms wrapped around her. Ethern's warm breath cascaded over her neck. At some point, he'd returned to her, even if she hadn't noticed.

"I won't leave your side again. I'll fight with you. I love you, Jessica. Together we'll change the future."

She turned in his arms and pressed a kiss to his lips. Her hand reached up and stroked at his cheek.

"I know. I feel the vision changing already just by opening the book. The magic is in me now, and I won't stop until Ciaran and Nuka are destroyed and the human's accept us for who we are."

CHAPTER SEVENTEEN

*E*thern hated the vision that had remained with him ever since he'd become a multi-shifter. It haunted his dreams, and he couldn't escape from it no matter how hard he tried. However, using it to reveal the future to Jessica had soothed him. He knew it showed her just how much the world needed her to be strong, and if she needed him in the dark days ahead, he'd be by her side the entire time, no matter what. Right now, though, he longed to be inside her—only intimacy could erase the vision from their thoughts.

He pushed her up against the wall behind them, their lips meeting in a passionate frenzy of kisses. His hard torso held her in place against the inflexibility of the wall. They were learning the flavor of each other's desire. It was consuming them both in an urgent need to feel something, anything pure and joyous, to alleviate all the pain that had engulfed their lives over the last few days.

The magic swirled around them again—their blue and red auras dueling in a tango to create vibrant purple hues.

Ethern tugged at Jessica's t-shirt, releasing it from the waistband of her skirt before tearing it from her body in one swift movement. He buried his head in her breasts, savoring the soft flesh there, while Jessica's hands teased his t-shirt from his jeans and stroked at the tautness of his torso.

He stepped back for a second to admire her beauty —he was a very lucky man. Jessica reached forward, and lowering the zipper of his jeans, she released his already hard and desperate cock from inside. He pushed his jeans and boxers a little lower down his thighs before lifting Jessica up and holding her against the wall in his strong arms. She parted her legs and wrapped them around his waist, and finding her core in an instant, he tore her panties from her body.

"Yes," she cried out as he pushed hard into her, in one long stroke.

It was bliss. Jessica was wet, warm, and welcoming all at the same time. He'd never known such longing, such pleasure. Her svelte legs wrapped tighter around him, bringing him closer, deeper within her. Her nails dug into the flesh of his torso still hidden by his t-shirt, and she let out low moans of sheer animal passion.

Ethern could feel the flames of passion sparking as his length propelled ever deeper, more mercilessly within her. Their hips rocked, backward and forward, moving together and making them one entwined, heaving body of desire. This union was raw, wrapped up in the vision they'd both witnessed. Neither of them knew what was coming next in this war. It would surely test them to their very limits, but together they could put a stop to Ciaran and Nuka's plans to destroy the world. He and Jessica had to believe in their strength, or they'd fail.

Ethern was straining against the burning need to empty his release deep inside her. They both surrendered completely as he drove powerfully within her innermost sanctum now awash with the liquid heat of her craving. Jessica finally abandoned herself in a fulfilling climax of pleasure. Her inner muscles gripped tightly to him like a vice around his length. It took him over the edge, and he climaxed with her name on his lips.

They both remained against the wall for a few moments until their breathing returned to normal. Ethern eased himself out of Jessica, immediately lamenting the loss of her warmth, and supported her while she lowered her feet to the floor.

"Wow." Jessica finally found her voice.

"I have to agree." Ethern kissed her one final time before tucking himself back in his jeans.

"I'm going to go and clean up. You make us some hot drinks," she suggested, looking at the book, "and then we'll get started. It's time to end this."

Ethern couldn't agree more. They needed to put an end to Ciaran and Nuka's schemes. He just had to hope that Jessica's decision to use the book would change the part of the vision he hadn't yet shown her. The part where he lost his life in the next few hours.

CHAPTER EIGHTEEN

*E*thern had done an excellent job of distracting her from the vision and calming her erratic thoughts. After her intimacy with him, Jessica went to her bedroom and had a long shower to further clear her mind. Then, having changed into jeans and a fresh t-shirt, she returned to her magic room to begin working on the spell.

Jessica stared down at the book she'd feared for so long, and taking a deep breath, she opened it again to the spell to bind dark magic. She studied the words and began to gather together the ingredients required, collecting a bunch of dried herbs from a box on a shelf and placing them on the table in front of her.

Methodically, she worked through the spell, mixing

the herbs as required with a little lavender oil to form a paste. The herbs contained a mix of lemon thyme, oregano. and sage, so it was quite potent.

The final ingredient required was a blue Miro flower—it wasn't commonly known about in the human world. She was relieved she'd collected a bunch and dried them several years ago. They were only found in a remote part of India at the top of a large hill surrounded by monkeys. It wasn't a pleasant place, and she really didn't want to return there any time soon. She retrieved one of the flowers from a pot of other unusual ingredients on her shelf and mixed the flower into the paste. The first part of the spell was complete.

She stepped back just as Ethern walked into the room with two coffees and some vegan oat cookies that Isobel had made earlier in the day. Isobel and Jane had gone into baking mode to keep everyone happy and relieve some of their worry about what was happening. It was working, just a little.

Ethern popped one in his mouth and quickly devoured it.

"These are good. I'm hungry."

Jessica raised an eyebrow at him. "I'm not surprised. You just fucked me almost into oblivion against a wall."

"Almost?" Ethern smirked.

"You'll just have to try a bit harder in the future, but

the world needs me at the moment, so make sure you keep holding back for now."

Jessica picked up the pot with the paste in and moved to the center of the room where she kept the area clear for performing spells. The only thing visible on the floor was the pattern of a pentagram drawn in permanent marker.

"It's a deal! As soon as this is over, we're going to be spending an entire month in bed together. There's a lot more of your body I want to explore. I really can't wait to see you wrap your mouth around my dick."

Jessica whimpered. "I like the thought of that, but I need to concentrate on this spell and not be turned into a sex manic." She knelt down on the floor as she spoke. "I'm starting to wonder if Kas is right, and something about this house is making us all go sex crazy."

Ethern was now sitting on a chair by the table she'd mixed the herbs on, and he took a mouthful of his coffee as he watched her.

"I'm not sure that's a bad thing. We all need a release every now and then— plus, if it's with someone you love, then it's even better."

Jessica looked up at him and smiled.

"I can't agree more. Hopefully, we can change the future so Kas can find someone of his own, and then everyone will be happy. I keep thinking back to

Morocco and Zahara in the vision. They're part of the next generation of the pack and to see them alone at such a young age…it's not fair. They deserve a better life for the heroic efforts of their parents. I'll never understand why Nuka is so misguided. I know Ciaran is just pure evil, but I'd like to think Nuka isn't. Maybe I'm wrong and he is. It's just that whenever I look at him, I see Kas. I suppose I'd like to believe there's at least one good bone in Nuka's body because I can never see anything malevolent in his brother."

Jessica dipped her finger into the paste and started to draw a design on the floor, matching the one she'd memorized from the book. She made sure the diagram of flames with stars around them stayed within the confines of the pentagram.

"I used to want to think Nuka had some kindness hidden away inside him, but when I saw the way he went after Selene, I knew he had none. He's done everything he can to destroy this pack and has never given up when he's failed. Now he's turned his sights on the world at large, and he'll not rest until he gets what he wants. The sad thing is he won't succeed. No matter what, we've seen the vision of his future. He's misguided to think the humans won't fight us in force. The scary part is knowing what they'll do when they're terrified of something different. It makes the human's strong. There are still so many divisions in the supernatural world. We'll never defeat them when we can't fight together as one when it's called upon. The problem is, it's nature to us, more so than the humans, to protect our own at the cost of others. I guess the humans are right on some scores when they look at the shifters, the animal instincts are still there."

"I never thought about it that way. I guess, being a Wiccan, it's different for me. I'm more of an in-between to the human world than the shifters are. I have powers, but I look human even as a witch."

Jessica finished the drawing on the floor and returned to the table to retrieve the Book of Shadows. Ethern handed her the coffee he'd brought her, and she took a mouthful of the now cooled drink. She followed that with a bite of one of the cookies before picking the book up and returning with it to the center of the room.

"As a multi-shifter, I've experienced more than most. I see the world from so many different points of view. From the tallest animal to some of the smallest, and everything in-between. It's been an experience. Selene seems to have taken to it naturally, but what I can do sometimes scares me a little. I feel like it's forced with me, and I was meant to be something else."

Ethern shifted on his chair. Jessica could sense an unease about him.

"What's wrong with the way you are? What else

could you be? Human?" She placed the book down on the floor beside her and searched Ethern's demeanor for any signs she could read to pinpoint what he was feeling.

"No, my human body was right for me at the time but not anymore. I feel most at ease when I'm performing magic like you. Maybe I've had more lives than I care to remember, and I'm an ancient druid or something. I could have been the original Merlin." Ethern tried to lighten the mood with a joke, but Jessica could still feel the fear coming from him.

"We could probably do with King Arthur on our side if you're able to resurrect him." Jessica laughed.

"He wasn't overly keen on the supernatural, though, remember?"

"Damn."

Ethern got to his feet and came to stand near where Jessica was still crouched on the floor. She rose up and stepped into the pentagram. He reached out and stroked his hand down her cheek, and she leaned into the affection.

"No matter what happens, I'll always be with you." Ethern gently lowered his hand down her neck and shoulder blade to rest over her heart. "I've never known feelings like this. Together we have the power to stop this. It's our destiny."

Jessica nodded. She knew he was right. This was

what needed to happen. Her deadly affair with Ciaran had led them down this path. She'd found the man to complete the triangle, and now she had to kill the apex of it. Jessica inhaled deeply and glanced down at the words in the book. She read through them once more. They were already memorized within her head, but she wanted to make doubly sure.

"I'm ready," she informed Ethern.

"I'll be here the entire time." He leaned forward and pressed a bruising kiss to her lips. "Remember that. Remember the feeling of me inside you. The goodness in our love will keep you grounded always."

"I will. I give you my word."

Tears started to tumble down Jessica's cheeks. She'd never been so scared in her life, but it was time to grow up and face the real world. Magic was her calling, and she was damn good at it. Ciaran Dunaid had made her feel second best by feeding off her. It was now time to show him just who the most powerful druid on the planet Earth was and put a stop to his reign of terror.

She stared straight ahead into Ethern's warm chocolate eyes as she started to recite the spell,

Spirits of the world beneath,
I call you forth to help me destroy
One who seeks to ruin this world for all—
Darkness can't rule in this place,
Only the light may shine—

Give me your strength,
Allow it to fill my willing body,
And give me the power to finish
What evil has been started.
Is mise an cumhachd,
Is mise an cumhachd,
I am the power.

Jessica's eyes filled with light, the pupils disappearing to leave only white in their place. Bolts of energy in blacks, grays and whites shot from the ceiling, walls, and floor, directly into her body. She could see concern on Ethern's face. His jaw was ticking, and she felt how much he wanted to step closer to help her. She shook her head to tell him she was all right.

She let the power take over her body. It surged through her, and endless abilities flashed in her mind. Spells she could only have dreamed about—she knew how to do them with no effort at all. The spell to allow the humans to hear the shifters in human form entered her mind, and she felt a big smile break out on her face when she realized what she'd been doing wrong all this time. She'd make that right as a point of urgency.

The energy grew in intensity. It illuminated the room so brightly she saw Ethern shielding his eyes, but it was when his skin changed to green and the tattoos appeared on his body she knew it had worked. The magic had called out to all those with abilities to tell them of a new power in the world to match the strength of Ciaran. Ciaran himself would now be experiencing what they'd felt the night he summoned the darkness to him.

The light in the room vanished, and she stepped out of the pentagram. Ethern stood before her in his druid form.

"It worked," he stated.

"It did," she replied with a smile.

Ethern rushed toward her and gave her a searing kiss on the lips. She savored every part of it like a woman starved of affection for years and years even though they fucked in this very room just over an hour before.

When Ethern pulled away from her, his eyes went wide.

"What is it?" she questioned, fearing something had gone wrong.

He reached to the side of her face and pulled a section of her hair forward. When Jessica looked, her tresses were no longer the color of night but the color of heaven, bright white.

"Ciaran is the darkness—you are the light, Jessica. We can stop this."

"We can. I feel it." Jessica placed her hand over Ethern's heart. "In here."

Before she had a chance to say anything more, Ethern collapsed in agony on the floor. He grabbed his head and screamed. Ciaran must be performing magic again, the other druids always ended up in pain when Ciaran was in the grip of a spell of a demonic nature. Before she could reach for him, the door to the magic room flew open, and Kas entered.

"Is Selene all right?" Jessica questioned.

"The same as Ethern." Kas cocked his head at her hair. "Er, that's different. If it's magic causing the pain, then why aren't you experiencing it too?"

"Because Ciaran can no longer reach me via the traditional methods."

Jessica knelt down beside Ethern and placed her hand on his head. The vision he was experiencing was projected into her but without the pain. Just as swiftly as he'd fallen to the floor, writhing in agony, Ethern stopped moving, and she rolled him onto his back.

"Rest." She kissed him before standing again.

"What's going on?" Kas questioned. A few of the other shifters from the pack had appeared at the door: Zain, Scott, Tyler, and Teagan.

"It's time to end this. Ciaran, Nuka, Samuel, and your grandfather have just landed in London. They're going to destroy the city and kill the royal family. You better shift if you don't want anyone to see your real identities."

Jessica held her hand up, and before the shifters had finished changing into their animal forms, they were already moving through the air toward London.

CHAPTER NINETEEN

*E*thern felt like he was floating. The good magic now surging through him was vastly different to the pulse of bad magic Ciaran sent out whenever he performed a spell. This magic was just as powerful but not painful. The agony that had gripped him earlier had been emanating from Ciaran and was a warning of what he was about to do. It would be horrific, but Jessica now had the power to stop it.

Ethern gingerly got to his feet and allowed his druid form to take over. Jessica had already left for London with some of the shifters, but he was going to join them as soon as he checked on the other members of the pack. He transported himself into the lounge. A few of the councilmen were watching the television, and Ethern saw Jessica land in London with the others, directly in front of Buckingham Palace. A flag flew high in the sky indicating the Queen was home, and Ciaran and Nuka were already bearing down on the royal residence.

In the lounge, Brayden was helping Selene to her feet.

"I need you to take me there." the snow leopard beta of the pack demanded.

"I will," Ethern promised.

"And me." Selene allowed her body to change into druid form, the rotund shape of her stomach evident in the dress she was wearing.

"And us." Several of the councilmen stood up.

"If we outnumber them, then maybe we have a chance to stop them," one of them added.

"We're coming as well." Katia and Jackson got to their feet.

Emma was the only shifter in the room who hadn't responded yet. She silently stood up from where she was cradling her twins, Morocco and Zahara, and handed one to Isobel and the other to Jane.

"I'm never one to miss out on a fight. Look after them." Emma kissed the top of her children's heads and instantly shifted into her powerful lioness form.

Ethern heard a voice in his head. It was Lily. The bear shifter who now lived with her partners, the human, Kingsley, and wolf shifter, Hunter. They wanted to help as well, and he wasn't going to disappoint them. Without another moment's hesitation, he called forth his magic, and with Selene's support, they transported the remaining shifters to London.

When they arrived, Kas was already standing up to Nuka, warning his brother not to carry out his plan and to return to Canada instead. The younger twin was having none of it, though, and ordered Ciaran to start his destruction of the city.

Ethern watched in horror as Ciaran fired off two energy bolts toward the palace. Thankfully, Jessica was able to stop them.

"Enough," Kas shouted again, although the humans couldn't hear anything, but the roar of a mighty polar bear. "Nuka, this isn't the way."

Police sirens bellowed around them. Some of the humans ordered them to stop while vans full of police officers with guns descended on the scene. It was obvious to Jessica they wouldn't hesitate in killing the shifters if it came to it. She waved her hand in the air, and a protective shield descended around them. Nuka, Samuel, Ciaran, and the Lincoln's grandfather were on one side, supported by a few members of Nuka's pack, and on the other, the Glacial Blood pack: Kas, Brayden, Selene, Scott, Emma, Tyler, Teagan, Zain, Jackson, Katia, and Jessica along with Lily, Hunter, and some of the councilmen. All in animal or magical form so they couldn't be recognized when this was over.

"There's only one way, Brother," Nuka responded, "and this has to be it. I will not hide away any longer, because they fear us. We're the stronger race. They should run and hide from us. This is our planet too. Why should we have to hide who we truly are?"

"The way you're doing it is showing them they should fear us. Why destroy symbols of human hope? It's wrong. We're supposed to demonstrate to them how kind we are, not prove them right by hurting them."

Nuka let out a bellowing laugh.

"You might not hurt them, Kas, because you're weak, but I will. I won't let them control me."

Nuka cocked his head at Ciaran again. The druid instantly sent out a burst of energy toward one of the van's containing armed officers. Jessica wasn't quick enough and couldn't stop it from blasting into the side of the vehicle and ripping it in two. Ethern gasped at the loss of human life. These were men and women who served their country—men and women who might have families. Anger rose inside him. He knew he should stay back. He'd seen this scene play out so many times in his head, but he couldn't.

"Stop this, Nuka," Ethern ordered and took his place at Kas' side in the standoff against Nuka's pack. "This is not the way, no matter what you believe. Go home, we'll open communication channels with the humans. You can be involved in the discussions at all times. Don't destroy anything else. Don't prove to them we're the dangerous wild animals they believe us to be."

"Says the councilman who came here as a druid rather than an animal." Nuka sneered at him. "Tell me, Ethern, were you scared to come as an animal? Too much risk of being put in a cage and experimented on because that's what will happen if we attempt to talk to the humans. We need to destroy the symbols of their hope and freedom, and when they're left with nothing, we'll rid the world of the humans too. That's the only way we can freely walk the Earth as shifters." Nuka paused, and turning to his beta, he ordered, "Do it, Ciaran."

The druid flew up into the air and landed on top of the palace. He ripped the flag from its pole and threw it to the ground before commanding the building to rise into the air. Jessica flew up, and Ethern watched as she forced Ciaran to abandon his plan and engage in a fight with her. Magical energy blows were traded between the two. Nuka reared up on his hind legs with a loud roar before landing down on all fours and racing toward Ethern and Kas with the rest of his pack following on behind him.

Kas stayed rooted to the spot while Ethern made a

decision. For the next part of the fight, he needed to be an animal. His favorite was a leopard, so he allowed his body to change to the large spotted cat. Nuka took on his brother while their grandfather headed straight for Ethern. The two exchanged blows. A polar bear had a lot more weight behind his fighting technique, but Ethern was nimbler and managed to get a strike in to the bear's side. The polar bear roared as the sharp claws sliced his flesh. Ethern didn't want to kill the man. No shifter wanted to murder unless it was a necessity for food.

Ethern ducked as a fire blast flew over his head. Samuel was using his fire abilities to protect the man who once inhabited his body. Ethern jumped out of the way and back into druid form. The Lincolns' grandfather stepped back from the fight, and Samuel took over. Ethern formed a protective shield and deflected the fire being blasted at him. He cast a spell to turn fire to ice, and the flames died the instant they came near him. Samuel roared in frustration and turned his focus onto one of the other councilmen when he saw him approaching.

Ethern took a moment during the ensuing chaos around him to see what was happening to Jessica. She and Ciaran were still trading blows. He promised her he'd be at her side, so he rose into the sky and toward the roof of the palace.

"You won't win, Jessica. You've never been stronger than me. It's why I chose to feed off you," Ciaran taunted her.

Ethern felt the anger rising within her. She shot off two wayward blasts. One slammed into the building they were on, causing some of the stonework on the west wing to crumble.

"You'll pay for everything you did to me, Ciaran. I can't believe I thought I loved you. I was a fool. I know what true love is now, and when your rotting in hell, I'll be alive and happy with Ethern."

Jessica was not controlling her emotions or the power within her. She'd revealed something to Ciaran that Ethern knew the evil druid would be more than happy to use against them. Ethern stepped closer to Jessica. He needed to ground her. He allowed his aura to leave his body and flow into hers so she could feel him.

"Remember I'm with you," he spoke only to her, to her very soul. "I always will be. You *can* do this, Jessica. You know the spell. Say it. Stop Ciaran before he can do anymore damage, bind his magic so he can no longer use it."

Jessica breathed hard, her chest moving quickly up and down. He felt the conflict within her.

"I want to kill him, painfully, Ethern. I want to strip

his skin from his body and watch him bleed out. I want to hear him scream."

"No you don't, because what you felt for him was never love. He's nothing to you. Us, we're everything. I love you. Fight against the urge to destroy. It's not who you are. It's not who you'll ever be."

"I can't," Jessica pleaded with him. "Help me."

Ethern stepped closer to her. He placed his hands on her hips and allowed his magic to combine with hers. Ciaran cocked his head their way, trying to figure out what Ethern was doing. "True love, Jessica, is good not evil. Feel me, I'm with you. Now bind his magic. Save your friends…" Ethern fell quiet for a few moments before adding in a whisper, "Save me."

A strong blast of energy from Ciaran sent them both backward and falling from the roof of the palace. Ethern knew this feeling. He'd experienced it before in a vision—he'd seen himself falling like this, so many times before. His aura and magic were keeping Jessica grounded. He couldn't use it to save himself. Jessica flew high up into the sky, but he kept falling, faster and faster, until he hit the ground.

Everything hurt. He gasped in agony, metallic blood pooling at the corners of his mouth. His body turned back to human as Jessica looked down at him with horror on her face. He knew what happened next. He'd been preparing for this moment. It wasn't fair when he'd just found love. Fate was cruel. He was destined to die. He'd helped Jessica find the courage to save them all, but he was not to be rewarded for his efforts. He was fading, the breath within him flying away. He tried to speak, to spur her on, but nothing came out.

Jessica let out a blood curdling scream, and with all the power she possessed, still grounded by Ethern's magic and life, she sent a blast of magical energy toward Ciaran. Through his link to Jessica, Ethern could still see what was happening, and he watched as the blast of energy hit the vile druid directly in the chest and pushed him backward across the roof. Black tendrils of evil ripped themselves from Ciaran's body. The dark magic was leaving him, going back down to the underworld and taking all the magical powers he ever possessed along with it. He would be left powerless, a mere mortal—a human with only the knowledge of magic and a few basic spells. It was a worse punishment than death for someone who'd been in control of such greatness.

Jessica had fulfilled her destiny. She'd played her part in saving the world. Only time would tell, though, if it was enough. The Glacial Blood pack had dealt the first retaliatory blow in the war, but it had come at a cost. As Jessica came to his side to hold his hand, the fighting stopped all around them, and Nuka and his pack vanished. Now the world at large knew of the existence of shifters, and Jessica would soon be taking the Glacial Blood pack home to prepare for battle.

Ethern knew his last breath as a multi-shifter was here. The darkness of death claimed him.

He just had to hope his deal with the afterlife would be honored.

CHAPTER TWENTY

The rest of the Glacial Blood pack made their way back to the mansion, but Jessica couldn't, not yet. She needed more time at the grave of the man she loved. How could the world be so cruel? She'd found the one man who could complete her, and he was ripped from her arms. The hem of her black dress swayed in the wind. It was a stark contrast to her white hair.

The world around them was still in chaos, but she'd not been able to start trying to repair it. She was too deep in her grief and felt that any spell she performed would mean she'd lose a part of Ethern who still resided within her. His magic and aura had entwined with hers the moment he'd died. A few more days, and then maybe she'd try.

Kas appeared next to her.

"It's getting cold. Do you want me to help you inside?"

Jessica shook her head.

"I'll stay here a little while longer, thank you."

Kas knew not to argue with her. He bowed his head toward the grave of their dear friend Ethern Lennox, and he made his own way back inside.

"I need you, Ethern." Jessica fell to her knees, allowing the emotion to overcome her. "You promised me you'd be with me always. I know your magic is inside me, but it's not the same. I want you. Your body here next to me. I want to feel you and touch you. Have you make love to me. Why? Why do I have all this power, and yet, I can't have you? It's my punishment." She allowed her heart to break. Tears streamed from her eyes, and her voice broke with every word. "Why did you leave me? I hate you. You did this to me. You and that damn book. I'm going to burn it. Let it rot in hell. This isn't the way it's supposed to be." She fell lower to the ground and curled up in a little ball by his grave. "I love you. I love you so much. I'm sorry I couldn't save you. I failed. The book wasn't meant for me. I didn't lose my life to it, but I lost yours. I'm so sorry."

"You have nothing to be sorry for, Jessica."

She instantly recognized the deep gravelly voice and sprung upright in a sitting position.

"Ethern?" He was there in front of her. Was this a trick? Had she had a breakdown? She was seeing dead people now. "I think the grief is too much." She shook her head and rubbed her eyes, but when she opened them again, he was still there. "What's happening?"

Ethern knelt down beside her and took her hand. She felt his touch. It wasn't cold but warm.

"It seems I'm the man who can't die."

He pulled her closer to him.

"I don't understand. We've just buried you. I put you in the coffin. I sealed it with my magic," Jessica sobbed.

This must be a dream of some sorts. It couldn't be real.

"And that's what has allowed me to be here, my old body is buried, and my new one can now rise. It's a different form to the one before, but I'm here, Jessica. I promise you. This is real. I'm sorry I couldn't come sooner. It's been killing me, watching you grieve."

"You're real?" With her free hand, Jessica reached up and touched Ethern's face. She could feel solid flesh. "You're real," she repeated again.

"I am," he answered and pulled her into a searing kiss.

Her entire body exploded in a chorus of 'Hallelujah'. But then his words hit her.

"A different form? What are you, Ethern?"

Ethern smirked.

"I was wondering when that part would register. I'm a reaper. It's a deal I made with the underworld to save Selene. I promised that when I died, they would get my services. They kept their word, and I'm going to keep mine."

"You're going to collect the dead?"

Ethern nodded.

"It's not particularly pleasant. I can hear my bosses calling me now to get on with it, but I'm here. That's all that matters."

Jessica pulled away from him. She got to her feet and started to pace along the side of the grave.

"No, no. I can't get my head around this. You're here, but you're not. You're in the ground." She was so confused. Her head was pounding.

"Yes. I don't understand the mechanics of how it all works, but it does." Ethern tried to come near her again, but she stepped back.

"Elizabeth," she stated flatly

"What about her?" Ethern looked confused.

"One life, one love." She looked at the grave. "Another life, another love. This time it won't be me."

Ethern pulled her close. She tried to pull away, but he wouldn't let her.

"No, that life and this one is yours. I feel you inside

me, Jessica. I can't get you out of my head, even though I have a different form. The love is still there and stronger than ever. I don't know how the future is going to turn out, but I know I'll be with you every second of this life if I can. It's my last chance, no more deals. When I die next time, it will be the end. I'll die with you at my side."

"Together."

Jessica felt tears beginning to fall again. She was a mess at the moment. So much for the strong independent witch. Love itself had broken her, not hatred.

"Always," Ethern promised as he pressed another kiss to her lips.

When they pulled apart, they were in Jessica's bedroom.

"I didn't even feel that?" she exclaimed in shock.

"Upgraded magical abilities," Ethern boasted.

"Er…you're not here to collect me are you?" Jessica asked tentatively.

"No, I'm here to fuck you."

Without saying another word, Ethern winked at her, and their clothes disappeared from their bodies and appeared neatly folded on a chair in the corner of the room.

"Ok, this magic is better than mine, and I'm supposed to be all powerful at the moment," Jessica complained.

"You haven't had a chance to figure out what you can and can't do. I'm sure once you get the hang of it, you'll be able to do anything you choose. I won't be around all the time. I have to honor the afterlife by reaping, but I'll be with you when I can." Ethern looked sad. "It's going to take a bit of getting used to."

"I know," she reassured.

Ethern pushed her against the bed, and she fell back on to it before sitting up and saying, "I just remembered something you said the day you died."

"What was that?" Ethern questioned, stroking his hard length. Jessica reached out, and pushing his hand away, she leaned forward and licked her lips purposefully. "Fuck, I remember," Ethern growled.

Jessica moved closer to Ethern's cock and kissed the tip. She swirled her tongue around the length and back over the sensitive head before swallowing him deep into her mouth.

"It's as beautiful as I imagined." Ethern smiled down at her. "Totally worth coming back to life for."

"I should hope so," Jessica responded, playfully squeezed his heavy balls hanging down between his legs.

"Damn it, Jessica. If you do that much more, I'm going to come, and I've not tested the stamina of the reaper body yet."

"I hope it's good," Jessica mumbled around his dick as she brought it into her mouth again.

Ethern twisted his hand in her white hair and gently pulled her off him.

"Ok, you need to stop that. I want to be inside your pussy when I come."

Jessica nibbled at the edge of her lip,

"I like that idea."

She was ready for Ethern to take her. The truth was she'd been that way since she'd heard his voice again. She lay back on the bed as he placed himself at the entrance to her body and pushed inside her. She welcomed him joining her. There were no aura's twisting on the ceiling around them. The magic Ethern had was already inside her, keeping her grounded.

He pulled his hips back and then thrust inside her again. Jessica was home. She was with the man she loved, and she'd destroyed the man she hated. Ciaran would be licking his wounds. She'd taken everything from him but his life. It was perfect. Now she could concentrate on helping the shifters find a place in the world that didn't lead to the vision Ethern had shown her. She was worthy of being a powerful witch, and she wouldn't rest until she'd proved it to everyone, not just herself.

Ethern quickened his pace, and Jessica wrapped her legs around his waist and her arms around his neck.

She worshiped him with kisses. He wasn't dead. He was alive and giving her orgasms. The first one hit her quickly, and she allowed it to flow out of her in a chorus of singing birds. *That was different!* The next orgasm had snow falling all around them to cool her down.

Ethern buried himself deep inside her, and she felt him find his freedom again.

"I love you, Jessica. I don't know how it works for druids or reapers, but I want you as my mate, my forever. Will you marry me?" Ethern had stilled with his cock inside her.

"Of course I will. I love you too," Jessica cried.

"Doesn't anyone stay dead around here? Fucking and not dying is all that ever happens in this world." Kas moaned through the door. "I'll be off catching seals if anyone needs me."

Jessica couldn't help but laugh.

"At least some things are normal."

"Yes," Ethern responded with a smile before his face fell.

In the next instant, they were dressed, and he was taking her hand.

"What's wrong?" Jessica questioned.

"There's something I need you to take on and protect for me. Something big. The time is coming to use it, and we need to be prepared. Come, I'll show you."

Jessica took Ethern's hand, and with fear in her heart once more, she allowed him to transport them into the darkness.

EPILOGUE

*N*o matter how much he stared at the bones, Hayden couldn't bring himself to touch them again. Once was enough. They'd changed his whole life. Left him alone and not completely stable. The flash of what hid inside him, flitted over his eyes, lizard like in appearance. He subdued the beast once again. Now was not the time. He had to wait.

He looked up from the bones as Ethern appeared in the high ceiling cave. Hayden kept it dark, but Ethern swiped his hands through the air and lit magical lights on the walls. Hayden blinked at the sudden onslaught of brightness to his eyes. It was then he noticed the other person in the cave. She looked familiar. It was the witch from the Glacial Blood pack, but her raven black hair was now pure white. She'd taken the magic of the good inside her.

Hayden's hands shook with nerves. His time was getting nearer. It wouldn't be long now. The animal within him was restless and desperate to escape.

"How are you?" Ethern asked.

Hayden sensed a difference in his friend.

"What's happened?" Hayden ignored Ethern's question and replaced it with one of his own. "You're not a multi-shifter any longer?"

"How can you tell?" Ethern frowned.

"Apart from your sudden preference for black clothing, only you know the location of the cave. Even if you told Jessica, she wouldn't be able to teleport here. You brought her, and you didn't turn green with brown markings to do it. Your magic is different."

"Clever." Ethern perched on a rock near Hayden while Jessica stood by Ethern's side. "I died. We stopped Ciaran, but I lost my life. The afterlife held up their end of the bargain, so I'm doing the same. I'm a reaper now."

"Interesting. It's started then." Hayden nodded his head to Jessica.

"It's more than started. We're near the end now. It's do or die for a lot of people. Jessica is going to take over the responsibility of looking after you and the bones. It will be Selene's time soon."

"Selene's time?" Jessica interrupted at the mention of her friend. "What's going on, Ethern?"

"Sorry." Ethern got to his feet. "Jessica, this is Hayden Eckert. He's another multi-shifter."

Jessica put her hand out for Hayden to shake it, but he pushed himself back into the shadows. There was no way he was touching her or anyone else anytime soon. It was too dangerous, especially with the magic she held within her body.

"Er..." Jessica withdrew her hand. "Pleased to meet you."

"Same," Hayden grunted. "Does she know?" he questioned.

"No, not yet," Ethern replied, and Jessica looked at him crossly.

"What is going on? I don't like secrets, Ethern. You know that."

"I'm sorry." Ethern brought the witch into his arms. "You know a multi-shifter can change into any animal or magical being they've touched before?"

"Yes," she replied, looking between the two men.

"Well, these," Ethern gestured to the bones on the floor, "are dragon bones."

"Dragon?" Jessica questioned disbelieving. "They're mythical creatures. They're not real."

"They're real, all right," Hayden spoke up.

"Could you?" Jessica lowered her head and voice to Ethern. "Could you change into a dragon?"

Ethern shook his head. "No. A dragon is a powerful creature. Only one multi-shifter has done so and survived."

Jessica instantly turned her head to look at Hayden.

"Your eyes, Hayden. When we arrived, they turned to a lizard's for a brief moment."

He nodded. "But not a lizard's, a dragon's eyes."

Hayden got up from where he was sitting and walked to the largest part of the cave. Ethern pulled Jessica to him and held her close as Hayden started to change into a magnificent beast. Fifteen foot high with a wingspan of the same proportion. Scales of glorious turquoise and dark teal covered his body, and horns ran along his back, decreasing in size from his tail to his head. When he looked down, Jessica's eyes were wide open.

"Holy shit!" she exclaimed and tried to step forward to touch him.

"No." Ethern held her tightly.

Hayden started the transformation back to a human.

"In dragon form, it's difficult for him to control his beast. This is where destiny comes into play again. Selene will be the only one able to control it because she has Brayden."

"Selene? I'm so confused right now?" Jessica

scratched at her head. "How do the multi-shifters know all this?"

"We just do. It's a part of us, just like the visions are. I can't explain it," Ethern responded. Hayden could see his friend was in love with this woman. "Please, Jessica, I just need you to help me protect Hayden until it's time."

Jessica let out a long breath. "I'll do whatever it takes."

Ethern kissed her, and Hayden felt the ever present pang of longing in his heart. The amorous young couple turned back to him, and Ethern let go of Jessica's hand.

"I need to report to the afterlife and start my new job. Why don't you stay a while and find out more about Hayden and the dragons, Jessica? I know it'll interest you. Your magic should allow you to return home when you're ready, and I'll change the spell to allow you to come back here whenever you want."

Jessica instantly agreed, and Ethern left them alone.

"How long have you been here?" Jessica asked, perching on a rock while Hayden took his place back in the shadows, staring at the bones.

"Too long." He was an older man now. He'd continued to age during his absence from the world both in the cave and at the Reichstag. "Can I ask you something, Jessica?"

"Of course." She smiled warmly back at him.

"How is Molly?"

"What?" Jessica looked confused.

"These took me from her a long time ago," he said, waving his hands over the bones. "But I've never stopped loving her. I just want to know she's happy."

The End

Glacial Blood continues with Power of Myth coming November 2020. You can pre-order it by clicking this link —> https://amzn.to/2Bex5o4

ABOUT ANNA EDWARDS

Anna Edwards is a British author from the depths of the rural countryside near London. When she has some spare time, she can also be found writing poetry, baking cakes (and eating them), or behind a camera snapping like a mad paparazzo. She's an avid reader who turned to writing to combat her depression and anxiety. She has a love of traveling and likes to bring this to her stories to give them the air of reality. She likes her heroes hot and hunky with a dirty mouth, her heroines demure but with spunk, and her books full of dramatic suspense.

CONNECT WITH ANNA EDWARDS
www.AuthorAnnaEdwards.com
Newsletter: http://eepurl.com/cwxJ6v
Facebook, Friend: TheAuthorAnnaEdwards
Email: anna1000edwards@gmail.com

THE GLACIAL BLOOD SERIES

A world of shifters and witches, magic and mayhem, unforgivable lies and unbreakable love. A world where family is born not only through blood, but bond. With plenty of the threats to come—and a secret that remains untold.

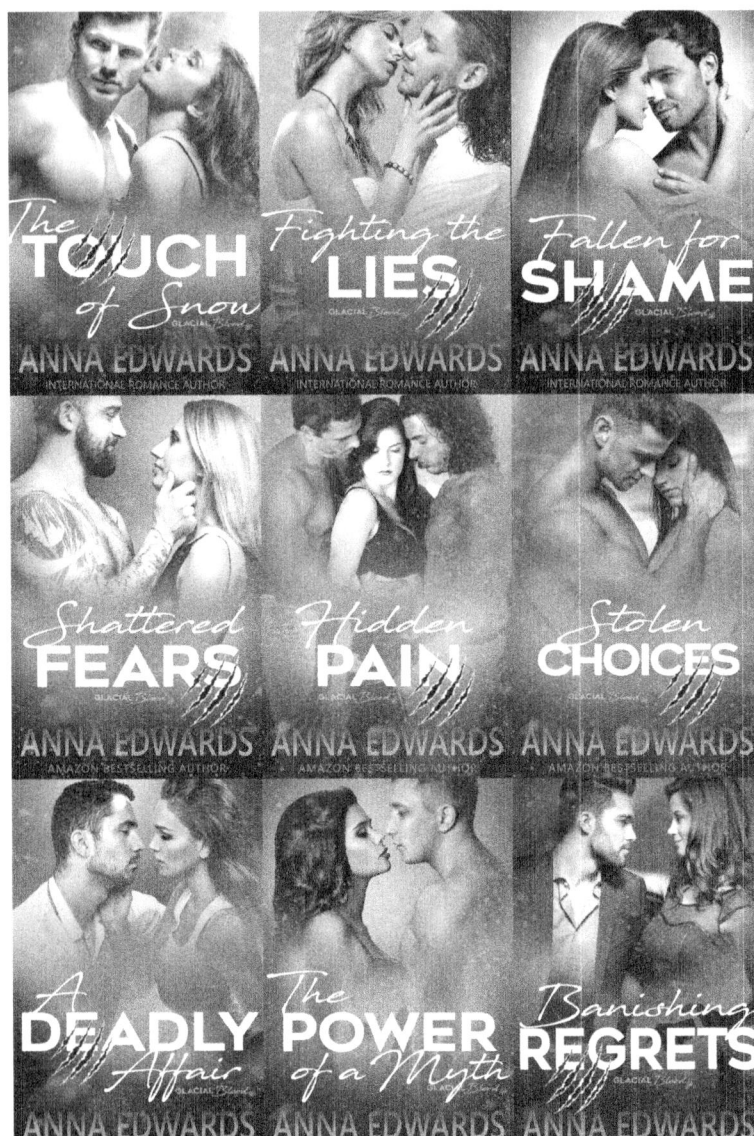

DARK SOVEREIGNTY SERIES

A complete dark and suspenseful series set amongst the elite of a London society intent on finding power in the wrong place.

Legacy of Succession

Tainted Reasoning

A Father's Insistence

SING WITH ME

SAVING TATE COLLECTION

Are you ready to meet the hottest new rock band on the planet?

Sing with Me by Anna Edwards, coming June 22nd

A With me In Seattle Universe Novel from Lady Boss Press.

Pre-order now

Amazon US: https://amzn.to/2X37NAy

Amazon UK: https://amzn.to/3bAvGog

Amazon CA: https://amzn.to/2WA4vWM

Amazon AU: https://amzn.to/3cDqQs2

Blurb:

Tate Gordon is the lead singer of Saving Tate, the hottest new rock band in Seattle. Having been mentored by music legends, Nash, for several years, the group are about to head out on their first world tour. Tate's excited, but he's struggling at the same time with the secrets he's been keeping. His friends don't know the truth about his youth or the confusion running through his head. Will Tate's past destroy everything the group have been working for when his past returns in a chance encounter?

Zoey Danson is a hot commodity in the record industry, and her boss wants her to travel with one of his top clients, Saving Tate, as they embark on their world tour. She's not entirely sure about being stuck on a tour bus with four famously horny men but mounting debts, thanks to her deadbeat mother, mean she doesn't have a choice.

When Zoey ascends the steps of the tour bus, looking hot and carrying a clip board with a full itinerary, sparks instantly fly between her and Tate. Can these two keep it professional, or will their instant attraction lead to an explosive disaster no one could have foreseen?

Sing with me is part of Kristen Proby's 'With me in Seattle' world and the start of a brand new rockstar romance series from the author, Anna Edwards.

The amazing summer launch lineup includes books from these AMAZING authors:

Melissa Brown

Anna Edwards

Bailie Hantam

Leigh Lennon

Stacey Lewis

Julie Prestsater

Jen Talty

Mary A. Wasowski

All of these stories stand alone, and are tied to the With Me In Seattle Universe in some way. You do not need to read them in any order.

https://www.ladybosspress.com/with-me-in-seattle

I'm drowning in a sea of nothing, and this is an experience that will only come once in my lifetime.

Printed in Great Britain
by Amazon

77904486R10129